White Wine
&
Wild Rides

Connie Cox

White Wine and Wild Rides
Copyright 2013, Connie Cox
All rights reserved.

ISBN-13: 978-1-940601-03-8

Single Titles

White Wine and Wild Rides
Contractually Yours
Taking Flight

Harlequin/Mills and Boon Medical Romances

The Baby Who Saved Dr. Cynical
Return of the Rebel Surgeon
His Hidden American Beauty
When the Cameras Stop Rolling…
Christmas Eve Delivery

DEDICATION

To everyone who dreams of walking on the wild
side.
What are you waiting for? Permission?
You've got it! Do it now!

CHAPTER ONE

Selina Ramirez exhaled as Phoebe, the mistress of the studio, tugged on her corset strings. Selina's breasts plumped and threatened to spill.

Phoebe studied the overflow. "A little toupee tape should do it."

Lengths of fluttery tie-died silk and strips of metal-studded leather lay across every surface of the San Francisco couturier's workroom waiting to be turned into wearable works of art. Poster-sized stylized watercolor washes of a woman either riffing on an electric guitar, crooning into a microphone or strutting on a stage leaned on easels around the room. In its center, two triptych mirrors formed a mini-room that reflected into infinity.

The money that would change hands today would keep three designers and four seamstresses in rent money for the next six months.

Best of all, Selina Ramirez, escapee from Castor, New Mexico—population one thousand, two hundred and thirteen—would be paying the bill. No, the money wasn't hers. All that lovely money was from her employer's bank account. But that only heightened the moment.

Who would have thought that, eighteen months ago, Selina would be live-in personal assistant to the hottest pop star in the world? Working for Blair was turning out to be much more rewarding than her last job of thrusting tooth-picked chicken samples at unwary pedestrians while wearing a red yarn wig and oversized blue striped bloomers.

Being the same body type, the same size, even the same height as Blair were the attributes that had sealed the deal on Selena's employment.

Blair detested fittings. Not so Selena, who had grown up wearing clothes from charity bags. Her prom dress had come from the lost-and-found box at the hotel where she'd cleaned during high school. Now she was the recipient of Blair's continuous closet purges. Not only were her clothes the chic-est hand-me-downs in the world, they were custom-fit, too.

Not bad for a high school graduate whose only money handling experience had been pocketing left-behind change as a hotel maid and ringing up charge cards as a ticket seller at Cliff's Amusement Park in Albuquerque.

She took a deep breath as if she were about to belt out a high note. The boning cut into her bottom ribs. "Loosen it a bit around the ribcage, please."

Phoebe worked some slack into the laces. "How's that?"

"Much better." Selena scrutinized herself under the stark lights. "It needs something. A splash of color, I think?"

"Red?"

Selina imagined Blair's spiky white-blond cut instead of her own waist-length dishwater-brown ponytail.

"How about an inset of electric blue?" She sketched out a design on a napkin slightly damp from the green tea Phoebe served her clientele. "What do you think?"

"Nice." The voice over her shoulder was much deeper than Phoebe's. But then, Eric Saunders's voice was much deeper than most men's. "And the design's not bad, either."

Selina laughed, of course. She always laughed at Eric's corny jokes. She could say that she was paid to humor her employer's friends, and, with many of them, she earned every penny. But Eric was different. Eric actually spoke to her, not through her. His business savvy had landed him a feature in Forbes, but his charm had garnered him a spot on Vogue's list of most eligible bachelors.

He gave her a wink to remind her that it was all in fun. As if she could forget. Even if his grin gave her the same thrills as the last big drop on the New Mexico Rattler at Cliff's, she knew she wasn't even in his theme park. Everyone knew Eric was a big player. Teasing was just his style.

He tickled her neck with the stiff ends of her ponytail. "I'm not too sure those khaki shorts evoke the mood you're going for, though."

"Oh? What would you suggest?" She sent him a sideways glance, full of fun and flirtation.

She enjoyed a good tease as well as the next girl, and Blair encouraged familiarity among her staff and friends. One big happy family made Blair happy and Selena did her best to oblige.

Eric examined Selena inch by inch, while she returned the favor. He was such a hottie. This job really had its perks.

He rubbed his chin as if in great contemplation. "I'm thinking about a skirt like a cheerleader wears."

"Like a short pleated skirt?"

"Yeah, with those panty things under them."

"You mean bloomers?"

"They're not really called bloomers, are they?"

"Yup."

"Now, that almost kills the image." Eric gave a deprecating shrug. "I'm just a guy, so what do I know?"

Phoebe cleared her throat. "You know, a kicky little pleated skirt in a butter-soft leather is not such a bad idea." She bit her lip then plunged ahead. "It's swingy and sexy, but full enough to, well, to...."

"To hide generous thighs?" Selena patted her own curvy derriere.

Eric acted as if he was scrutinizing her through a monocle. "If I may be so bold, mademoiselle, your thighs are absolutely perfect, as are all your various parts and pieces. And may I also say that you have the finest mind I have ever encountered." His poor imitation of a French accent made his words even more over-the-top.

Eric made it easy to smile, even if, deep down, Selena wished he were at least a little sincere. But she adored his absurd humor that matched her own so well.

"I bow to your superior fashion assessment. You are quite the expert, I understand, monsieur." She curtsied carefully. It wouldn't be politic to flash her employer's best friend with her overflowing décolletage.

"So I've been told, mademoiselle." He faked modesty by ducking his head and looking up through his long, dark lashes. "I would not be so unseemly as to argue with a lady."

"Well, sir, if you are not here to argue, then why have you come?"

Eric dropped the accent and moved back a pace, getting down to business. "Blair called. Her appointment's running long, so she asked me to pick you up."

They exchanged worried glances, but Selena quickly broke eye contact and turned her attention back to Phoebe. While Phoebe had been discreet so far, you never knew when she might decide to sell a tid-bit like Blair's doctor visit to the press. Too often, the urge to gossip surpassed even the large profit margin that superstars produced.

She dug her phone from her bag and checked the dates of the upcoming photo shoot. "Can we get the modifications done by Tuesday after next?"

Phoebe pulled up a screen on her laptop. "I don't know about that Tuesday. The following Friday, maybe?"

"Hmm. That Friday won't work. We've got to have time for a final fitting before we pack for shipping. How does Wednesday look? We'll pay premium." Selena felt pride every time she realized how fully Blair trusted her.

"Is ten o'clock okay?"

"Ten it is." Keeping Blair on schedule was worth the extra bucks. Selena tapped the appointment into her calendar along with the note about the extra charges and handed Blair's credit card to Phoebe. Blair had a thing about owing people, so she paid up front as often as she could.

Phoebe did her thing with the card and reverently handed it back. "I so enjoy your visits."

"Me, too." Selena accepted Phoebe's social hug, not as tense as she once had been about making full body contact with a virtual stranger. Blair had such a warm and open style with everyone she came into contact with, that everyone expected her personal assistant to follow suit. Selena did her best to meet expectations. She had been hugged and air-kissed more in the last eighteen months than she had in her whole previous lifetime.

As soon as Phoebe left the room, she whispered to Eric, "I didn't see Blair before I left this morning. How's she feeling today?"

Eric frowned. "Pretty bad. And the welts are worse, too. I don't think there's an inch of skin that's clear. The itching is making her nuts."

"If you're here, how is she getting back home?"

"Dominic is driving her."

Selena stopped worrying. Dominic was the most committed bodyguard she'd ever seen—not that she'd seen that many. But she knew first hand how Blair's innate kindness inspired loyalty.

"Let me change and I'll be ready." She slipped behind the wooden lacquered screen to exchange the leather corset for her navy tank, a new acquisition courtesy of Blair's spring cleaning, since that particular shade of dark blue wasn't Blair's color. It enhanced Selena's darker complexion perfectly. The simple knit top matched her curves, even down to the armholes and straps, like it had been made for her. Since she had stood in for the fittings, it literally had been custom-tailored to her. Damn, she loved her job.

The way Selina saw it, her job description was to take as much load off her boss as she could. She stood in for fittings, managed Blair's schedule and melted into the woodwork when required. Beyond her own healthy paycheck, she earned awesome perks like her rent-free apartment, a great wardrobe and Blair's trust and friendship. And today, it seemed, she'd scored Blair's handsome escort as well.

This year alone, Blair had already completed a twenty-city tour, two videos to debut around Christmas time and a multitude of public appearances, including carefully staged glimpses at parties and awards ceremonies, all designed to keep the paparazzi interested.

That's where Eric came in. Enough above average in looks to be a backdrop in the photos but not so much to outshine his date, hip enough to wear the right clothes well, but not so hip that he could get his own tickets to the chichi affairs he loved to attend. He loved the glitz and energy, the late nights and the mad dashes in search of frenzied fun. And he loved Blair. He claimed it was completely platonic but the gossip columns said otherwise.

But those rumor rags also said he'd loved a good two dozen other high-profile women, too, depending on however they could twist and turn their latest photo scoops, despite Eric's assertion that those girls had just wanted to have fun.

Selina vacillated between believing him and believing them. While she'd seen Blair and Eric at the breakfast table together, she'd never seen anything more—not that she'd looked for it. She would swear that Eric hugged *her* in public more often than he hugged Blair. Of course, the hugs were just for fun. Deep down, she was honest enough with herself to want to believe but to realistically doubt that his and Blair's relationship was nonsexual but, in the end, it didn't really matter. She didn't play where she worked. Continued employment always got shaky when personal and business relationships collided.

She emerged from behind the screen to see Eric scrutinizing the watercolor of Blair and her guitar.

"You want to drive through the burger biggie for your favorite haute cuisine?" Eric's light gray eyes sparkled as he ragged her about her plebeian taste. No trendy gourmet fare for her.

Her mouth watered for her favorite high calorie indulgence, a chocolate shake with an extra shot of syrup. Over the top of the screen she yelled, "I'll go anywhere with you for fast food."

She emerged from behind the screen, smoothing down her ruffled hair with her brush and replacing the rubber band. Then, with a wave for the receptionist, she exited through the door that Eric held so gallantly for her and studied the steep steps that led down to Eric's chili-pepper red Lamborghini Gallardo parked at the curb.

"Allow me." Eric took a firm grip on her elbow. Together, they walked down the narrow uneven steps. "Nice shoes."

"Thanks." Her canvas wedges lifted her butt, lengthened her legs and inspired Eric's hand on the small of her back. The advantages of her less-than-sensible shoes plainly outweighed their disadvantages.

Luck was with them. No parking ticket fluttered under the wipers. The San Francisco police department must have better things to do today than give out tickets in the Haight.

Eric rushed to open the door for her and held out his hand so she could gracefully sink down into the low slung seat. His old world manners always made her feel pampered and protected. The first time he had held a door and ushered her in front of him, she had felt awkward and gauche. But she had gotten over it as quickly as she had recovered from any hesitancy about the luxuries Blair expected her to enjoy.

These times would make good memories.

Eric jack knifed his six foot frame behind the wheel and reached for his sunglasses. "Top up or down?"

"Down, of course." From under the seat, she grabbed the baseball cap that Eric kept around just for her.

They zoomed over the Golden Gate Bridge north toward Mill Valley and Blair's home. The wind whipped too fast for conversation under shouting volume so Eric flipped on the radio. The Beach Boys belted out Little Deuce Coupe. He gave Selena an apologetic look, cranked up the volume, then burst out in off-key song. She leaned back her head and laughed, adding harmony as out of tune as his melody. Life was good.

In Sausalito, Eric slowed down to turn at In-N-Out Burger. He studied the menu below the squawk box and asked her, "What'll it be?"

She decided to be at least a little bit sensible. "A cheeseburger, mustard, no mayo, no fries and a diet Coke."

"Diet? What are you trying to do? Waste away right before my eyes?" He considered the menu. "I'm getting a vanilla shake. How about you? Chocolate? Extra syrup? I know it's your favorite. Don't you want to reconsider?"

She looked at him, amazed. "How did you know?"

"Would you believe me if I told you that I remember every word you have ever uttered?" He flashed a grin, typical playboy-style, no matter how badly Selena pretended to see something more in it.

She answered with her own cheeky smile, making it sarcastically lopsided to cover up any inappropriate desire that might sneak through. "Uh, no, but it's a nice thought."

He spoke their order into the speakers and then pulled around to the window, where Eric thrust a couple of bills at the cashier and she thrust a sack full of food back at him. Then they headed for the roadside park. Eric angled the car so they had a great view of the water.

He reached for the radio knob. "On or off?"

"Off, thanks." Selena breathed deeply of the ocean air. The surf crashed and swelled, sending waves of power through her veins. Before moving to San Francisco, the closest Selina had ever gotten to the ocean was watching 90210 reruns. Back then, Selena would have never imagined that she'd be sitting next to an incredibly handsome man in his superfine car, eating hamburgers while watching the Pacific Ocean crash a few feet away.

They slurped and munched in companionable silence. If she had three wishes at this very moment, she wouldn't use them. Nothing could make this day any better. Well, nothing but a soul-sucking kiss from Eric. And that was beyond wishing for. Blair had given her the perfect life and she intended to enjoy the hell out of it.

She let a smile blossom on her face as she breathed in pure happiness.

Eric noticed her grin and returned it. "What? Share?"

"You've got to promise not to tell."

"Cross my heart."

"When I answered Blair's ad in the paper, I thought I was applying for a nanny's position."

"No! Really?" Eric's brow creased as he thought about it. "I helped her write the ad. I guess it might have sounded more like she was looking for a caretaker than a personal assistant. She was lucky to get both in such a great package deal, especially at the price she could afford to pay back then."

"Thank you, kind sir."

Selena had been hired just as Blair got a foothold on the charts. The pay had been low, but the job came with room and board and that had been worth gold to Selena.

She had been sharing living space with her ex and his new squeeze. The arrangement hadn't made for the most comfortable of surroundings, especially since she'd been relegated to the couch in the one bedroom apartment and they had all shared a single bathroom.

The little studio apartment behind Blair's house was cozy but all hers.

Between then and now, Blair had hit the top of the charts fourteen times, had the highest grossing concert tour in the country and had started her own clothing line.

"How was your mini-vacation at Big Sur Boardwalk? Still riding your roller coasters solo?"

"Yup. It took me three tries but I finally talked the attendant into giving me the back seat all to myself. There are taller woodies and there are faster woodies, but there's not a woodie out there that shakes like the Giant Dipper. Riding that bad boy definitely makes my pulse race."

"Woodies? Are we still talking about wooden roller coasters? I can just see you batting your eyelashes at some helpless teenage boy." He faked a falsetto. *"But it's so much better in the rear."*

Eric's sexual implication made Selena blush, even as she laughed at his razor-sharp wit. "I don't know if it was the eyelash fluttering as much as the twenty I slipped him."

"Oh, one of those 'anything for money things', huh?"

That one cut.

"Something like that," she said as she diligently kept her smile in place, even though the old wound still burned. Eric had no clue about her past history and he never would.

Still, he must have seen something in her face. "Selena, I'm sorry. That was in poor taste."

"Don't go all formal on me now, Mr. Prim and Proper. I thought it was funny." She watched him from the corner of her eye. "I wore the T-shirt you gave me."

"Yeah? Get any second glances?"

"A couple. Mostly from guys who wanted to join the club."

The shirt had been a joke, a gag gift that Eric had designed and printed for her birthday. Over a graphic of a classic wooden rollercoaster the shirt read, *Everyone loves a woodie.* Under the picture, the shirt said *Join the Woodies Thrillseekers.*

Eric pointed a limp French fry at her. "You told them the club was exclusive and membership was limited, didn't you?"

Was that judgment in Eric's eyes? Didn't he know her better than that?

"What do you think?" She winced at the sharpness of her tone even as he did the same.

Of course, he knew her, the grown-up version of her. But he didn't know about her high school years and he didn't need to. The only reputation that haunted her was the one inside her own head.

To soften her attitude, she leaned over and whispered in her sexiest voice, "I want your fry." And opened her mouth, waiting.

As always, Eric took her mood swing in stride. How could any woman not adore this man?

He fed her the French fry, his fingers brushing her lips.

She licked her lips, tasting salt. "Mmmm. Something magical happens when the lowly potato sizzles in hot grease, don't you think?"

"Not nearly as magical as when a beautiful woman's lips suck my fingertips."

When he drawled his words like that, Selena could almost believe he was serious. She needed to remember that flirting was just a part of his goodtime boy repertoire. Nothing personal meant.

Now was not the time to let the conversation stall. *Come on, Selena, think about something other than mouths and nerve endings.* "If the wine business ever sours, you'll make a perfect..." she was going to say gigolo, but something in his eyes made her change it at the last second to "...actor."

She would have missed his lightning-fast reaction if she hadn't been hyper-attuned to him. Apparently, she wasn't the only one with a sensitive side.

He covered well as he answered, "Acting, huh?" Did you know my grandmother was an actress? She bridged the gap between the silent screen and the talkies."

But she still caught his edge. Too polished. Too smooth. Too overly bright.

Ignoring what he didn't want her to see, she kept the conversation going. "Now I understand where you get your flair for the dramatic.

"Moi? Dramatic?" He slung the back of his hand against his forehead as he widened his eyes and faked shock.

As expected, and because the sparkle in his eyes made her smile, she giggled.

Slowly, his fake shock transformed into an expression she couldn't interpret, drawing her in so that she had trouble thinking. There it was. The charisma that seduced all those women into hanging on his every word. Nothing personal. She had to remember that.

Selena pulled the baseball hat tighter onto her head, shading her eyes, to break the heavy connection. "The glamour years, right?"

Eric bent his head to his straw to slurp the last of his drink.

When he looked back to her, that charm was safely locked away and he was, once again, Selena's easy-going escort, giving her a ride to help out his best friend, Blair. Nothing more.

"Right. The glamour years. Grandmumsy was one smart cookie. She bought land for the vineyard in the thirties, because it reminded her of the vineyards in Italy where her maternal grandfather used to farm."

"And now you're a world renowned producer of high-end vino."

Eric shrugged into the compliment. "For a boutique vineyard and winery, we've done well. Of course, when Blair's video for White Wine, Red Roses and Thorns hit the airwaves, sales went beyond prediction. Who knew that our Chardonnay, when dribbled in the right places on a bare body, would inspire so many folks to want our wine as well as Blair's albums?"

Selena hummed a snatch of the double platinum song under her breath. "That was one hot video, wasn't it?"

"Yup. She had just finished it when she hired you. To keep it under budget, she shot it in our barn. I haven't been able to think of that tractor as a simple piece of work equipment since then."

"Everyone's still speculating about who the naked guy was. It was pretty clever film making to show only a silhouette and shadowed shots of his hands on her." Selena waited for Eric to confess.

With just a touch of imagination, Selena could imagine herself in that video taking Blair's place. She stole a glance at Eric's fingers loosely cupping the gear shift knob. Realizing that her transfixed gaze was none too casual, she quickly adjusted her focus to his face. His eyes smoldered as they met hers. He couldn't know what she was thinking, could he?

"I'm sworn to secrecy." How could any man's voice sound so low and velvety?

To cover her reaction, she took the lid off her shake cup and downed the last swallow in a noisy slurp.

Chocolate pooled into one corner of her mouth. As she licked it off, she saw his eyes widen.

"Did I spill?" She dabbed at her lips, then her chin and nose for good measure.

"It's not..." Eric looked down.

"Oh, no. Not the shirt." She followed Eric's glaze. Bad move. She could feel herself harden through her bra. Yup, there they were, the twin peaks.

She crossed her arms, which only plumped them up.

"No spills yet." Eric grabbed his shades from the sun visor, slid them over his eyes then deliberately looked out at the water. The beginnings of a blush crept up his neck. "Are you ready?"

Yeah, she was. Ready, willing and able. But Eric was off-limits. Which only called into play the forbidden fruit issue. Still, she couldn't help finding his blush adorable.

She licked her lips and said in her most vampish voice, "When you are."

As her reward, Eric flushed even brighter. He looked back at her, then deliberately focused just left of her shoulder instead.

He was such a gentleman. Blair was so lucky.

He balled up the sack and wedged it under his seat. "Buckle up, then."

Using a bit more gas than necessary, he pulled back onto the highway toward Mill Valley and Blair. The temperature started to drop as the mid afternoon sun headed behind the clouds. Selena rolled up her window to shield from the draft.

"Do you want the top up?" Eric asked.

"No. I'm fine. I just wanted to get out of the direct blast." She grinned at him. "There's not enough sun in San Francisco to make me want to shut out a single ray when it decides to shine like this."

"I guess our weather is a bit more overcast than your hometown."

"And a bit more dramatic in the scenery department, too." She pointed to the steep drop-offs on either side of the rocky, winding road and the ocean off to the west. "I grew up in the desert. Sun, heat and miles of dust. Unless it snowed. Then sun, cold and miles of snow."

"Do you miss it?"

"Not today."

As they neared Blair's estate, Eric punched the gate control and sent the wrought iron monstrosity creaking open on its hinges. He slowed to turn onto the drive and a camera flashed beside them. From out of the bushes popped a photographer.

Eric waved and shouted a friendly "Hello, there."

Selena waved too, and an explosion of camera flashes left bright spots dancing before her eyes.

Everyone in Blair's entourage knew to fully appreciate the attention. Media played a big part in her success and she was always gracious, even when a photographer caught her at less than her best. Fame didn't happen overnight and then keep itself alive. It had to be deliberately fed with a 'candid' shot at the club or an exuberant sound bite from a trendy red carpet. With her new clothing line launching her summer line-up in a few weeks, keeping the buzz high was more critical than ever.

Selena looked back over her shoulder as the gates swung closed. "Won't that photographer be disappointed when he figures out I wasn't Blair?"

"I don't know if he got enough of a shot to make out who you are."

"I think that was John. If so, he'll make up something." She giggled. "As long as he doesn't morph my photo to make me look like a two-headed goat or an alien from Pluto, I don't care."

"I think you would make an adorable goat."

"Goes with the stubborn chin, I guess." She stuck her chin out.

He flicked it, then ran his thumb across her cheek. "I don't know if goats can have dimples."

He pulled the car to a stop in the circle drive by the front door.

"My grandmother called them angel's kisses."

His gray eyes darkened as he looked into her brown ones. "Lucky angel."

When he looked at her like that, she had a hard time remembering that he was Blair's and that she was just the hired help.

But then, a shadow blocked out the sun. She looked up to see Dominic standing beside her door, waiting for her.

"Blair has bad news."

CHAPTER TWO

If anything could comfort Blair, it would be the love and concern she received from the friends who surrounded her. And, right now, she needed a lot of love.

Blair's face had puffed so much that her eyes had swelled to a squint. Her fingers, her toes, even her tongue felt thick and clumsy. Red blotchy patches came and went over different parts of her but the itching and aching in her shoulders, back and knees stayed constant. Her head and her heart felt just as miserable as her body.

While her oversized Minnie Mouse T-shirt and bleach-spotted gym shorts weren't standard pop-star issue, they didn't restrict or scratch. Comfort clothes, Dominic had called them, when he'd helped her into them.

"I've got hives." Blair winced as her voice came out watery. She had meant to be brave and resigned about it, but she was scared.

"Oh, Blair, no!" Selena's stricken expression showed she understood the impact of the whole situation.

Not for the first time, Blair was thankful that she'd gone with her instincts when she'd hired Selena. No one else could suit her better. She just wished that Selena would look past their employer-employee relationship and accept the friendship that Blair knew could blossom.

Blair shifted in the bed and tried to adjust her pillow. Dominic reached behind her and tugged until she gave him a smile. "Thanks, hon."

Expressionless, arms crossed over his huge chest, he resumed his position standing against the bay window frame that looked out over the pool. He was another one in her life who was determined to keep himself boxed into the role he was hired for. At least in public.

And then there was Eric. Her best friend and, most especially, her sanity-keeper since her world had gone so crazy with fame and fortune.

"Aren't hives caused by allergies? Can't you get a shot or something?" Eric scratched at his neck, caught himself and looked sheepish. "Sympathy itching, I guess."

"Not mine. No shellfish or margaritas to blame this time. My doctor says they're from nerves." Blair's sigh came from way deep down. She'd worked so hard for so long and, now, this was the result.

The down duvet cover felt like it was smothering her, so she pushed at it. Before she could make much progress, Dominic pulled it off the bed and draped it across her grandmother's cedar chest that stood at her footboard.

Earlier, when Dominic helped her change and tucked her in, concern had darkened his eyes to aqua. But they had changed, as they always did when anyone else was around. Now, they were an emotionless, flat blue. It was a good damned thing she loved him so much. His mercurial behavior would drive a casual lover batty.

"The recovery is the biggest problem. I've got pills for the swelling and the pain and the itching, but they might not help at all. My doctor says the only real cure is rest and she doesn't know for how long." The pain in Blair's heart equaled the pain in her swollen feet. She swiped at a tear with a welt-covered hand. "Oh, Selena, what am I going to do."

"You'll take naps, of course, and get well." Worry was digging two creases between Selena's eyes, in spite of her forcefully cheerful tone of voice.

"But so many people count on me." A blur of faces stretched across Blair's mind, faces that depended on her success for their next paychecks.

"It can't be helped. You must rest. At least you're into your promo schedule now and not your production schedule. You'll just have to make that high-priced PR rep earn his pay." Selena had her phone in her hand, scrolling through phone numbers and appointments. "I'll call him tonight and set up a meeting for tomorrow morning. And you, young miss, will stay in that bed and make a dent in that stack of delicious paperbacks you haven't had time to read."

Selena was all business now. Brisk and efficient as usual. Her calm, matter-of-fact voice of reason did much to settle Blair's nerves. If anyone could make this work, Selena could. She was such a survivor.

Blair let herself lean back against her headboard and relax. "Thanks, Selena. You're so good for me."

Selena gave up a distracted half-smile in acknowledgment of Blair's affirmation, then paused in her scrolling to look up at Eric. "Blair can't go to your party this afternoon."

"I kinda figured that."

Eric was the dearest friend Blair had ever had. Attending the launch for his new Pinot Gris was the only thing he'd ever asked of her. Through all the years he'd supported her and all the tears he'd wiped for her, she had to let him down now. "I am *so* sorry Eric. I know how much this means to you."

"It's okay, Blair." His whispered kiss on her forehead did nothing to relieve her anxiety.

Then he sighed deeply and sent dramatic puppy-dog eyes in Selena's direction. "I'll just have to go all by myself. Unless someone," he winked, "will do me the honor of accompanying me."

Aha! Eric's genius *did* tend to surface just when he had everyone thinking he was a regular kind of guy. Blair felt stupid for ever worrying about him. She watched as he turned the situation into his advantage.

"Me?" Selena looked to Blair as if asking permission. It was the first time Blair had ever witnessed Selena being indecisive.

"Of course, you!" Blair smiled, despite her swollen lips. For the first time today, she felt better.

Eric had had a thing for Selena since the first week she'd joined the staff, but Blair hadn't been able to convince him to act on it.

As always when it came to Eric and women, Blair had to suppress the urge to wrap her hands around the neck of his gold-digging ex and squeeze until all that lovely settlement money was squeezed out of her. But now, with Selena, Blair had hope. Finally, he would make his move.

She sat up a little higher against the pillows. "We'll just follow the original plan but with Selena taking my place. Dom will drive you up to Sonoma and then he'll come back for you after the party. Okay?"

"I don't think you should be left alone." Selena moved in closer to Blair.

"As if Dominic would ever allow his security team to leave me by myself." She didn't care that contentiousness had crept into her voice. She'd fought against the constant attention on more than one occasion and today she was sick and had a right to be cranky. "And, tonight, Dominic will personally stay by my side. Won't you, Dom?"

"Sure." Although his answer was monotone, Blair detected the faintest hint of emotion flicker behind his eyes. A breakthrough! Although she couldn't have said whether her goading or her enticing had evoked it. Still, given time, he might finally let someone other than Blair see his human side.

She grinned, feeling like a happy marshmallow. "See, no problem there."

Selena bit her bottom lip. "But I don't have anything to wear."

The laugh that burst from Blair didn't make her chest her a bit. "You've got my whole closet at your disposal."

"Oh." She looked at Eric, doubt in her every move. "I don't know anything about wine."

"Neither does Blair. All you have to do is remember the five s's: See, Swirl, Sniff, Sip and Savor."

"But what am I supposed to be seeing, sniffing and savoring?"

"That doesn't matter. Just nod and say something like, 'What a delightful aftertaste', and look like you know a secret that's made you very happy and you're not sharing. The moment you get that mysterious look in your eyes, everyone in the room will want to share your secret. With any luck, they'll think my wine puts that special look on your face."

"You're betting a lot on my acting abilities."

"No, ma'am. Once you taste our new Pinot Gris, you won't be able to help having a look of bliss on your face."

Not without a bit of wistfulness, Blair watched the interplay between them. They didn't even know what they had together. Before she could stop herself, she cast a searching look at Dominic. Tall, dark and dangerous was all well and good, but a bit of public flirtation would be nice on occasion, too. She realized they were both looking at her. Had she made a noise? Had they asked her a question?

"That settles it, then. Selena will go in my place. Thanks, sweetie. Knowing you will take care of everything makes my mind much easier."

Sure, Eric could handle his own launch party, and had already several times over. But this was the perfect time to nudge Selena through that foggy wall she'd built around herself. Eric deserved a chance, and so did Selena.

Blair was not above manipulation when it came to her friends. If she got caught, she would blame it on the drugs.

"You, Eric, need to scoot. It wouldn't be polite for your guests to arrive before you. And, you, Selena, need to get dressed. You've got the run of my closet, of course."

Panic lit Selena's eyes. "My hair? What should I do with my hair?"

Eric paused in the midst of his chaste goodbye kiss to Blair's forehead and straightened to look at Selena. "You have beautiful hair. Just do whatever you normally do with it."

"Uh, thanks." Selena reached up with a hesitant hand and smoothed her ponytail. Her nervous movement revealed how much Eric's compliment had affected her. As he exited through the doorway, she recovered her aplomb. "It's an outside affair. I'll need an outfit with a hat."

"Do I have a hat?" Blair tried to remember what she had in her closet, but all those clothes ran together. As long as the sleeves didn't get caught in her guitar strings, she didn't really care what she wore. If she didn't have Selena to dress her, she'd still be wearing jeans and a stretchy sequined top for every appearance.

"Yeah, in your summer collection. Remember that adorable little hot pink and aqua baby-doll dress? It's got a sunhat with it. I could wear it with those mile-high wedge Mary Janes we ordered from Juicy Couture last week. They're perfect for a patio party. Then when the sun starts going down, I can add the white Pashmina shawl. But...."

"But what? It's perfect!" Blair gave into her urge to scratch a welt on her neck.

"Are you sure? That outfit just made its runway walk last week. It's the line's signature piece and it hasn't even gone into production yet. I don't want to upstage your debut in it."

"To tell you the truth, I don't think those bright blues and pinks do much for me. You'll do much more to make that dress look good than I will. Besides, the dress <u>was</u> custom-fit for you."

"Well, okay, if you're sure." Selena sent her a sideways glance. "What had you planned to wear?"

Blair grinned. "I don't know. I had planned to ask you before I got dressed."

Dom pushed himself away from the wall. "We had planned to leave here in forty minutes. Do you want to keep on the same schedule?"

Blair glared at him. "What's wrong with being fashionably late?"

He glared back. "Nothing, as long as Selena doesn't mind missing the popping of the cork."

"Eek! Forty minutes?" Selena ran through to Blair's dressing room. Hangers slid back and forth and a cabinet door banged, then Selena returned, dress, hat and shoes in hand. She rushed for the door. "Forty minutes, Dom. I'll be ready."

Blair rolled over and reached for the phone on her nightstand. "I've got to call Eric."

"Whatever." Was that a twinge of exasperation in Dominic's voice? It wouldn't be a bad thing if he were a little jealous of Eric every now and then.

Blair dialed Eric's cell and listened to it ring.

Eric was a good catch. A great catch, in fact. Before she met Dom, Blair had often wished that she and Eric could feel more than siblingish toward each other.

When she'd first hit the charts and Eric had made the Vogue list, they'd tried to be more. It had lasted two miserable weeks until they both realized it wouldn't work out. In fact, it had been so bad, their friendship had barely survived.

After their failed experiment, they'd made a pact to protect each other from the skanks that tried to take advantage of their celebrity by pretending to be a couple. After all, a girl needed friends as well as lovers, and Eric was a good friend.

Eric drove toward Sonoma but his thoughts were back in Mill Valley.

Until he and Blair had become a pseudo-item, he'd dated a lot. Everyone knew the rules. No heavy stuff, no ties, just grins and giggles all around, then a diamond necklace to end it all.

But Selena was different.

The first time he'd seen her, he'd had to remember to breathe. He had been sure his reaction was a fluke, an anomaly that would fade. Besides, she was employed by his best friend. What would happen when it ended? And these things always ended, didn't they?

The more time he spent with her, the more time he wanted to, needed to, be near her. Now when she glanced at him, his heart skipped a beat. When she smiled, his world raced around him. When she brushed against him, his body ached to rub against her. But it wasn't just physical closeness. Proximity, he could handle.

But she did something to his head—not just the little one throbbing between his legs.

He craved to be near her, to breathe the air she breathed, to feel the warmth of her fill all the empty places inside him.

You're pathetic, Eric.

His phone buzzed in his hip pocket.

When he saw Blair's pic on his display, he thought about ignoring her, but he knew from experience she wouldn't go away. They'd promised each other a long time ago that neither of them would ever leave the other alone. Blair had taken it more literally than he had.

"Hello?"

"Hey, you. It's me." Blair was trying to cover feeling miserable with a happy voice.

He'd let her get away with it. Sometimes illusions were as close as a person could get to the real thing. Having a Hollywood director for a father had taught him that at a young age.

"Uh-huh. That's what caller ID is for."

"With that deep voice of yours, it's a shame you can't carry a note."

"Need something, Blair?"

"Don't worry about shoulds and shouldn'ts tonight. Go with wants and needs, okay?"

His stomach tightened. Did she know or just suspect? Could he act his way out of this one?

"Eric? Still with me?"

"I don't know what you're talking about."

Her long sigh carried too many emotions he didn't want to think about. But overlaying it all was disappointment.

"Don't do that, Eric. We're friends. And friends don't lie to each other like that."

"I'm not—"

"You're not what? Lying to me? Then you must be lying to yourself." In the background, Blair's bed creaked. "What happens deep inside you when you hear her name? When you think of her?"

"Who?" he asked stupidly.

"Selena," she said and let it hang, as Eric's whole body tensed with unreleased energy.

His pulse raced, and not because Blair was calling him on his bluff. Yeah, Blair knew him too well.

An offhand smile from Selena made his whole life brighten. He'd even neglected his work so he could appear to be casually dropping in to visit Blair just for a glimpse of Selena. What would happen if he admitted to his need to be near her?

"Not going to happen."

The growl in his voice would make anyone else back off. But not Blair. She hadn't got where she was by backing off.

"Come on, Eric. You were willing to arm-wrestle Dominic for the privilege of picking her up from the couturier's shop this morning."

Too easily, Eric remembered that he'd almost lost all control when he'd seen Selena's silhouette as she'd undressed behind the screen at Phoebe's. Then, when she'd nibbled his French fries and her lips had touched his fingers he'd had to fight to keep his head from exploding. Yeah, both of them.

He drew in a breath, trying to make it steady. "Be practical, Blair. Selena works for you. You're my best friend. What happens if Selena thinks she has to be nice to me? I've seen it happen." Actually, he'd lived it—been the result of it—when his starlet mother had met his high-powered father and eight and a half months later....

The marriage hadn't outlasted the pregnancy and his mother never got her big break. Although she'd certainly got the pay off.

"Selena knows better."

"So maybe it wouldn't be so blatant. Still, there would be awkwardness. She hasn't given any indication she's even interested in me."

"You're both idiots." Blair blew out a breath. "Someone has to blink first."

This wasn't just about Selena.

He couldn't do it again, couldn't go beyond grins and giggles. He'd learned his own personal lesson too well. He'd been so young and naive, like Selena was now.

Jaded was good. Jaded was survival.

And Blair was stubborn.

He tried logical reasoning. "And when it ends, then what?"

"How do you know it will end, Eric? How do you know love can't last forever?"

"Happily ever after? That's just a fairy tale, Blair. It always ends." He wanted to be wrong so badly. He'd give up his inherited fortune to be wrong. Barely keeping the pleading edge out of his voice, he said, "Give me an example where it doesn't."

Blair was uncharacteristically quiet on the other end of the line.

Just as we was about to ask if she was still on the line, she said, "There's got to be a happy ending in all this. All the songs say so."

"Lyrics aren't real. They're just words that rhyme. You know that better than anyone. You write them."

Eric gave a fleeting thought to Dominic, the muse for Blair's music and the perfect example of love unfulfilled.

"I hurt for you, Eric. You're so wary. And you have good reason to be. But not everyone is like your parents. Or like that woman you married. Or like any of those women you date, either."

"You're making my point for me. Selena doesn't know the game. She's not a player."

"And neither are you."

"That's not what the tabloids say."

"And the tabloids are always right, right?" Blair did sarcasm better than anyone he knew. It wasn't her words but her tone that sliced through the hype. But that didn't change anything with Selena.

Before he could remind her of that, Blair talked over him. "Yes, you've been with scores of women. Maybe I should be more accurate by saying you've scored with scores of women. But you're not a player, either. You're just a guy who wants to win the game of love even when you think the dice are loaded." She laughed at her own turns of phrase. "I need to put that in a song, don't I?"

"Dedicated to me, of course."

"Who else?" The name Dominic hung heavy in the silence before Blair blew out a breath.

"It's just a party, Eric. Just a party that I can't go to, so my assistant is standing in for me. That's all Selena is thinking about. Don't worry about shoulds and shouldn'ts tonight. Show her a good time, for both your sakes, okay?"

What would it be like to let down his guard and enjoy Selena's company the way he wanted to for just one night? One night out of a lifetime. That wasn't too much to ask, was it?

"Okay."

"I expect a full report in the morning."

"I don't kiss and tell." Eric shot back without much thought.

"No, you don't have to. The rumor rags do it for you. But both you and Selena are used to that. Don't let all my hard work of having hives just to set you two up go in vain."

"Hives on purpose just for me, Blair? I really do owe you one."

"Not just for you. For Selena, too." The covers rustled over the phone line. "And there's no debt between friends. That's what you've always told me, right?"

"Right." Eric blinked and looked around him. It was a good thing he made the trip to and from Blair's so often his car knew the way. He'd given absolutely no attention to his driving. "Tell Dominic to take good care of you."

"He always does." Too many undertones coated Blair's voice to sort them out. Too many complexities Eric didn't want to think about. Too many layers to try to understand.

The only complexities Eric wanted to contemplate had to do with understanding the layers of the wine he would be presenting tonight.

Wine, women and song, each wrapped in complex layers to protect the heart that gave it substance. He had one of the three figured out, which was more than most men could claim. He should be content, right?

CHAPTER THREE

Blair replaced the phone, then leaned back against the pillows with a deep sigh and tried not to wriggle, since that just made her itch more. No distractions meant she was no longer able to avoid thinking about all the plans that would have to be canceled due to her hives.

Her career had been called meteoric. Was she really only a shooting star? Was this her burnout?

No! Her career was her life. She kicked off her covers as her temperature rose. She would not let her own body keep her from the dream she had fought so hard to make happen. Just how did someone keep from stressing out over a stress-induced illness?

Picking up her mood, Dom fidgeted with the curtains, cranking them open to stare down at the pool, then closing them again to darken the room. "Too much light? Not enough?"

She attempted a calming breath to keep the edge out of her voice. "The light is fine, sweetheart."

Dominic was a sharpshooter who could take off a fly's wings at four hundred yards, a martial arts expert who could paralyze a gorilla with a single blow, a commander who could plan a strategy to keep an excited crowd of two hundred thousand from ravaging a band of eight clueless musicians. Who would have ever guessed that he was also a lover who was too edgy to sit still because he felt her pain?

How could he keep so much hidden in public when he was so obvious about his feelings in private?

She'd heard his explanations—his excuses— before, and they were total bullshit. Why wouldn't he just embrace what they had and be okay with it?

But, right now, they had each other and that's what she would focus on. Not tomorrow or next year or next decade, but today, as he let his love shine through his eyes.

"Could I get you anything? What can I do?" His eyes, once again the color of the Mediterranean, clouded with worry. He hovered over her, waiting for an answer that would put both of them out of their misery.

"You could kiss it all better."

His eyes brightened at the task, but then they saddened again as he studied her. "Where? What doesn't hurt?"

"Hmm. Let me see." Blair watched him squirm as she let the anticipation build. "My ear isn't swollen."

"Your ear, huh?"

"Uh huh." With pudgy fingers, she pushed her hair back. "Do your best, lover-boy."

"Who you callin' boy?" He kicked off his running shoes and climbed onto the bed, careful to make it rock as little as possible. Then he held himself over her on his hands and knees.

Blair felt so deliciously trapped and protected. "I'm feeling better already."

"That's what I'm here for, baby. To make you feel good."

His lips tickled her ear as he spoke, sending a shiver through me.

"Cold?" he asked.

"No, getting hotter by the second."

He traced along the edge of her ear with the slightest pressure of his tongue, barely touching her, making every nerve ending scream in ecstasy.

"Good?" His voice, deep and quiet, dropped down into her center, awakening the faintest of pulses.

"Yes." It was more of a hiss than a word.

He smiled, satisfaction and mastery stamped on his face.

She reached up and threaded her fingers through the hair at his neck. Every so slightly, she let the tip of her pinkie trace through the baby fine hair at his nape, the sole place on his whole hard body that was sensitive. Under her thumb, she could feel his heartbeat, hard and fast.

"How about you, Dom? Are you hot for me?"

Above her, his eyes darkened and the muscles in his neck strained. He sucked in air then blew it out again. The warmth of his breath made every nerve ending in her come to alert.

He whispered in her ear, "This is for you, sweetheart. Not me, this time."

"I'll share." She lifted her hips, grazing his pelvis with hers through sheets and jeans. A definite bulge grazed back. "This might work better without so much between us."

"But you're..."

She put her finger across his lips. "Take them off. Now!"

He rolled over and pushed off his jeans while she scrambled to free herself of the sheets, her gym shorts and T-shirt.

Kneeling over her, he ran the palm of his hand over her beaded nipple. Her skin pebbled at his touch.

"I don't want to take this trip alone. Join me," she reached for him, wrapping her hand around his fullness and squeezing the way she knew he liked. "This is an ache you can make better."

His eyes took on the depths of the sea and she fully intended to drown in them.

His arms trembled above her, transmitting shivers to every cell in her body. Still, he held himself over her, so very cautious. "Slow down, sweetheart. I need to be careful."

His finger traced her nipple. She had to move, had to arch her back under him. Nothing else mattered but his touch on her skin.

"No. Not careful. Deep. Fill me." She was empty without him. And knew, on a level much more basic than thought, that she would only be whole with him inside her.

"Need you now." Wrapping her legs around him to pull him closer, she guided him down in no uncertain terms. As always, unless her safety was at risk, he gave in to what she wanted.

As he brushed her clit, white-hot sparks radiated, sending an exquisite quivering ache through every nerve ending. More. She needed more.

He hovered over her, barely inside her. She thrust up, but he caught her hip, then millimeter by excruciating millimeter, lowered himself down.

"I want all of you." She wrapped her arms around his neck.

He looked down into her eyes. "You've got all of me. Heart, soul and body." Then he eased himself up, even slower than he had gone down.

"Yes." Blair convulsed around him, her world spinning wondrously out of control. Tears streamed from her eyes and streaked down her face.

Above her, Dom held himself rigid, strain in his face, then released as he pulsed to her rhythm. Eyes closed, head back and mouth slack, he exhaled and bliss reflected from his face. As he fought to get his breathing under control, he looked down at her and smiled that little-boy smile that only she got to see.

She patted the pillow beside her and he rolled over onto it. He propped himself up on an elbow and studied her with such approval, she almost forgot about the hives.

"You are so beautiful when you flush like that." He trailed a callused finger down the valley between her breasts, then down to her belly. "God, I love you."

"Me, too." She moved his finger away from her stomach. She knew he'd made the gesture unconsciously, but his desire for babies crept out in his body language even when he didn't say the words. It was a secret longing he'd let slip not too long ago.

Regret swamped her. Regret and shame, knowing she wanted Dom on her terms, wanted to have it all her way. Her own instinctive reaction had put a barrier between them.

If only she could answer yes. But she couldn't, not without resentment.

No babies, no marriage, not now. How many female pop singers had lost their fan bases the day they'd said, 'I do'? Too much of her popularity was image, an image that Selena, Eric and Dominic had all helped her build, and one she planned to keep for a while longer.

"Later," she'd promised. Dom hadn't asked when.

Still, as she twined her fingers through his, a degree of sadness flickered across his face. Or maybe she just saw her own sadness reflected in his eyes.

Dom brushed the hair from her face and kissed her lips, gently and chastely. "Try to rest, sweetheart. I'll be in to check on you as soon as I drive Selena to Eric's party."

He took his clothes into the bathroom to dress. She studied the shadows across her bedroom ceiling, then finally rolled over and covered her head with her pillow. When Dom came out to kiss her goodbye, she feigned sleep.

Dom stood in the doorway and watched Blair try to keep her breathing deep and regular. He wished he'd never told her, never admitted that he wanted sons and daughters. But she had wanted to know and he could withhold nothing from her. And he couldn't help what he wanted, any more than she could help what she wanted.

He could wait. He would wait, forever. Because a family with anyone else was unthinkable. Blair was the key to his life, to his future, to his world.

But, for now, they all had to keep up the illusion that told the world that Eric was her boyfriend. While a bodyguard boyfriend might be so common it was a cliché, Dom couldn't do what Eric did to promote Blair's career.

Hell, without Eric, there might not be a career. He was the one that had given Blair the break she needed when she needed it. And he was a true friend to her.

Eric had the means to give her whatever she needed. He'd taken her into his own home and put her into his grandmother's care, got her fed and rested, then pulled strings and got her some studio work. When she gained a bit of polish, he'd hooked her up with a star-maker and she'd been rising on the horizon ever since.

Jealous much, Dominic? He mocked himself. *Yes, much.*

As much as he hated doing it, he had to be grateful to Eric for rescuing her from that creep she'd been hooked up with, the one who had almost killed her.

She had been young, just out of high school, when she'd headed to the city. Her small-time band had thought they could work their way up onto the nightclub circuit. Only problem, nobody had realized that Blair was too young to play in the bars. They had been so naïve.

San Francisco had lead singers everywhere. All she'd had to do was take a stroll down Pier 39 and see how easily replaceable she was. So the band had contributed to the kitty to send her home, but she hadn't gone.

She'd thought that going home wasn't a good idea. Money was tight and, now she'd left, there was one less mouth to feed. Besides, she was eighteen, old enough to take care of herself. She'd thought she could get a job waiting tables or something. Instead, she'd ended up on the streets, singing for her supper and turning over her meager earnings every night to some creep who'd promised to 'manage'. He'd had her out on the street corners for hours singing and begging. Then he'd take her home, rough her up and start all over again the next day.

That's where Eric had come in. Eric had passed by her every day on his way to classes. He'd advanced from throwing a few dollars in her guitar case to exchanging a word or two until, eventually he'd started noticing when some bruises faded and others showed up.

Cool, collected Eric Saunders had actually punched out the creep who'd claimed he was 'managing' her. Eric's family lawyer had made it all neat and tidy. He'd even been able to turn the tables and have the creep incarcerated for kidnapping and slavery. It would be a while before he walked freely on the streets again.

Dominic checked his watch. Time for Allan, his night shift man and partner, to come on duty. He headed down the hall to one of the spare bedrooms outfitted as the control center.

Allan had been a military buddy. Allan's grandmother had known someone who knew someone, so they had done a couple of short stints on celebrity detail after their enlistment was up. The jobs had paid well and they were good at them, so they'd formed their own company, and, well, here they were.

The row of monitors in the command center showed nothing unusual. He fast-forwarded through the tapes of the last few hours, then slowed to normal speed to watch a rerun of Eric stopped at the end of the drive waiting for the gate to open.

That was one damned fine car.

The man had good taste in wine, in women and in song. He'd been the one to discover Blair. He'd probably saved her life. Dominic couldn't help but be grateful, even if he had to fight down envy to get there. He just wished it had been him.

But, then, there was so much Eric could still give her that he couldn't. Eric had the social graces, the sparkle and the gift of gab that Dominic couldn't seem to develop. The few times he'd tried, he'd caught himself glaring suspiciously at everyone. Dominic just kept the bad guys away. And there were lots of guys for hire with that particular talent.

The gate alarm buzzed a legitimate entry sound. The monitor showed Allan's truck easing up as the gate swung open. Once Dominic completed his chauffeuring duties for Selena, he'd offer Allan the night off. Since Dom planned to finish out the night in Blair's bed, there was no since in Allan sticking around, too. Besides, with the way things were turning sour between Allan and his current lady-love, he might want some extra time with her.

Allan's footsteps sounded heavy in the hallway. He was an excellent bodyguard, well trained, alert and with great instincts, but no one would ever compliment him on his stealth.

"Hey, Dom. How's Blair feeling today?" Allan's oversized baseball shirt hid an arsenal of weapons, which he was extremely efficient in using, but his real talent was his ability to scan a crowd and pick out a face among thousands.

"Could be better. I'm driving Selena to Eric's party tonight in Blair's place. I'll hang out in Sonoma until it's time to pick her up." Dom handed Allan the latest sheaf of letters from Blair's less stable fans to analyze. "A few of these are from the creep's old prison block. I've got their release dates jotted in the margins. Check out their profiles and put their photos in your memory banks, okay?"

"Will do." Allan glanced up from the letters. "Any word from the parole board about the ex's release date?"

"Not yet."

A warning bell at the back of the property dinged and the monitors swung to focus on the heat source. A herd of mixed breed dogs, all large and loud, ran toward the high pitched sensor on the fence, and a skinny guy with a camera stood frozen in place as they surrounded him. Smart man. Dominic would give him a few minutes to think about the hazards of trespassing before he called off the dogs.

Allan squinted at the monitor. "He's a new freelancer that's made a few sales to the StarGazer."

"I'll let him take a few photos of the dogs if he wants to. Might deter any other idiots who try to break in."

"Smile pretty for the camera." Allan's own grin was anything but pretty.

Dominic gave Allan his best scowl. "Check in on Blair every hour until I get back. She knows to expect you."

"Sure thing."

Dominic left to have a little talk with the photographer. He had a hard time treading that line between cultivating the press and keeping Blair safe from them.

CHAPTER FOUR

After her whirlwind dressing session, Selena wanted to slump into the deep leather backseat of Blair's black limousine, but the hat that successfully covered up her hasty ballerina bun kept her from doing it. She must learn to fix it in a French twist someday but, after her fourth attempt and with the clock ticking, she'd decided that today wasn't the day.

"Seatbelt on?" Dominic asked, checking the rear view mirror.

"Yup. All buckled in." Being chauffeured to Eric's party felt like being driven to the ball. But, while Dominic might be a rat in disguise, she would never be Cinderella.

She had expected to feel decadent, sitting in the back of the dark-windowed limo with Dominic up front when she could have driven herself. But she couldn't sit back and relax. If her driver had been Allan, she would be enjoying the heck out of this. While she couldn't put her finger on why, she was uneasy around Dom.

Maybe it was all the overdone muscle, or the way he could walk up behind a person and never make a sound, or that he hardly ever slept. He just seemed plain dangerous, a good quality in a bodyguard, she guessed, but a lousy one in a traveling companion.

He cleared his throat and spoke. "About Blair...."

Selena came close to jumping out of her skin.

"Sorry. I didn't mean to startle you." His deep-woods Southern drawl didn't sooth her frazzled nerves.

Of course, he'd seen her reaction. He saw everything. His eyes in the rear-view mirror seemed spooky, like they could pierce lead walls.

"No, it was...I was just, uh, just...." She searched for what he had originally said. "What about Blair?"

"I want to thank you for taking such good care of her."

Huh? "Yeah, sure. That's my job."

"I meant beyond the job. I notice the way you make sure she has downtime and fun time for herself, even in the middle of a tour. And you stand up to her, argue with her for her own good when she wants to overschedule, even bully her, like now with her hives. There are some who would advise her to load up on drugs and push on. And she might do it for love of her fans. She needs taking care of and I'm grateful that you do it."

Not only had Dominic never said so much to her at one time, but he'd never said anything remotely more personal than, *Nice day,* or *Be careful.*

What was this all about? When in doubt, be politically correct. Selena said the only thing that came to mind. "Blair is so loving, it's easy to love her back."

His gaze narrowed, then softened, "Yes, it is."

The next thirty-five minutes loomed ahead of them in heavy silence. The solitude of the big back seat gave her plenty of room to think about what might be the guests' reactions when they expected Blair and got her instead. She couldn't hold back a deep sigh. Contemplating her upcoming duties as Eric's replacement arm-ornament was heavier thinking than she wanted to indulge in.

Instead, she focused on the luxury of riding in a personal limousine, wearing designer clothing that had been custom-fitted and attending the launch party of one the most famous boutique wineries in California.

Appearing there as the date of one of the most sought-after bachelors in the world boosted this little foray into the once-in-a-lifetime category, and she planned to take full advantage of it. If only her high school class could see her now. She had been voted the girl most likely to end up as a hooker. Now she was surrounded by elegance that her graduating class of Castor High School hadn't even glimpsed in the movies.

The scenic highway turned into quaint country roads which then became a private drive. A massively landscaped flowerbed of brilliant reds and yellows flanked either side of the asphalted drive. A discreet wooden sign read, Saunders Estate, Vineyard and Winery, est. 1928. Several hundred yards past the sign, wrought-iron gates gracefully blocked their entrance. The gates were massive and sturdy works of art softened by huge, welcoming grapevine wreathes. Next to the gates sat a guardhouse that resembled a miniature Swiss chalet. Dominic rolled down his tinted window and held up Blair's invitation for the gate guard's inspection.

With a motion that was half bow and half salute, the guard waved them through.

Up and up they zigged and zagged, as the narrow private road took them past hillside plantings and stands of native oaks to emerge upon a carefully manicured lawn. The landscaping rivaled the famous gardens of royal palaces, again in a floral theme of red and yellow. Dominic eased past the Maseratis and Jaguars that lined the circle drive to park in front of the mansion.

The Cinderella scenario hit her full force as she gaped at Eric's home. Fairy-tale castle would be a more accurate description. The stone stairs stretched a city block wide at the bottom then rose and slightly narrowed to an entrance more imposing than most major European cathedrals. Two doormen, one blonde and the other brunette, both exuding movie star polish in their black evening attire, stood ready to sweep open the massive oak and ironclad double doors.

She didn't realize she sat staring until Dominic cleared his throat. "Selena, are you ready?"

He stood next to the open back door, holding his hand out to help her exit the car.

Ready? For this? "Sure. Why not?"

The moment she stood, her stomach flipped, her knees threatened to fold and her hands started to shake. Was this stage fright? Blair had confessed to Selena that she always felt like throwing up before each and every show she performed. If this was what she went through night after night, no wonder she had hives now.

Dominic kept his hand firmly on her elbow as she climbed the stairs. No doubt, he could feel her shake. At least he was back to his normal, nonverbal self so he didn't comment on it.

Selena took a deep breath and forced a wide smile. On with the show.

At the door, Dom released her elbow. "Midnight."

"Yes." They were back to one-word conversations.

With synchronicity, the beautiful men opened both doors and Selena stepped inside. Stained glass from three stories above her head cast a kaleidoscope of colors across the Persian rug that softened the stone entry floor. Lemon polish from the richly wood-grained paneling blended with the natural perfume from the four- foot-tall bouquet of freshly cut flowers set upon a Louis XIV-style mahogany and marble table.

A young woman in an elegant petal pink suit glided toward Selena. "May I take your wrap?" She held out her hand toward Selena's Pashmina.

As soon as Selena handed over the shawl, an older man appeared in his black tux and presented his arm to her.

"May I have the pleasure?" His voice was full-bodied as if he sang opera. The Major Domo for the evening, no doubt.

She nodded yes, although, for a split second she was tempted to say no to see how the duo would handle a breach in their carefully performed welcome. Now was not the time to indulge in the quirky sense of humor that had gotten her kicked out of her high school graduation ceremony.

With a stately gait, the Major Domo guided her past a large formal dining room and a comfortably arrange media room, which opened out onto a flagstone patio that seemed as expansive as a soccer field. The patio seemed to hang on the hillside. Down below, multicolored fields of grapevines clung to the steep terrain and rested in the valley. In the background a quartet played Some Enchanted

Evening. Notes from a saxophone floated across the room while the bass line underscored the sensuality.

The patio teemed with beautiful people, women in garden party dresses and men in button downs and pressed khakis. The trio closest to her turned and surveyed her from head to toe. The two women gave her a tight-lipped nod of acknowledgment, while the man was more expansive with his slight smile. Their welcome made the patio seem rather chilly despite the bright sun overhead. Hopefully, the wine would soon have them all warmed up a bit.

"Madam." With a slight tilt of his head, her hired escort excused himself.

Immediately, a pretty young man in a starched white shirt and black bow tie appeared next to her and offered her a glass of wine from a sliver tray. "Zinfandel?"

Selena took the glass, grateful for something to hold on to. But then she started doubting herself. Had she read somewhere that she should hold the glass by the stem, not by the bowl? Awkwardly, she adjusted her grip. What where those five s's?

What the hell. She swirled, slurped and swallowed. Should anyone ask, she was prepared to pronounce this wine cold, crisp and wet with an afternote of potent.

Wine always seemed to go straight to her head and today was no exception. Already, she could feel her eye muscles relax just enough to make her world out of focus around the edges.

She twirled the half-empty glass in her hand and scanned faces, trying to find a friendly breech in the closed crowd.

That's when she spotted him.

Eric. Surrounded by a half dozen beautiful women, of course.

Welcome sparkled from his eyes as he smiled broadly at her and saluted her with his glass.

She knew she couldn't compete with present company.

But then, this wasn't her competition, was it?

Still—damn, it was good to see him.

She was breathtaking. Eric couldn't look away.

The women he'd been flirting with began to fade into the background. Mere wisps compared to Selena.

He wanted to kiss away the worry lines on her forehead, he wanted to wrap her in his arms and keep her safe from anything that could bring on a frown. He wanted to make love to her, slow and gentle, under a blooming grape arbor in a secluded spot. And he knew just the spot to make her squirm.

He nodded, beckoning her over.

When she was near enough, he reached for Selena's hand and pulled her through the circle of women, ignoring their tightened lips and huffing sighs.

Instead, he stared at Selena, top to toe and back again. "Wow."

She did a pirouette for him, holding out her arms and inviting him to inspect.

Of course, he accepted the invitation.

She wore some kind of tie-dyed halter top dress and mile-high heels. She'd stuffed her hair under her hat so that the dress exposed her smooth sweet shoulders, her deep, deep valley with a hint of breast, and her long, strong legs. A mental image of those legs straddling him made him dizzy.

He shifted his weight and tried to discreetly adjust his stance.

Her glance skittered across him. She blushed. Every nerve ending in his body went on alert.

"Wow, back. But, then, you always clean up well." Her voice was light and teasing. The same as always.

Not the same reaction he'd had, but he expected nothing different. What would he do if she actually responded with the slightest sliver of interest? Would all appearances of civilization desert him? Would he sweep her off her feet and carry her away to his cave to have his wicked way with her?

Had he been standing there, staring at her for so long that she was now deciding he was a total idiot?

He blinked himself out of his fantasy to discover one of the women had broken away and was now leading Wilhelm Schmidt back toward their group while whispering in his ear.

Wilhelm raised his eyebrows, then focused in on Selena like a heat-seeking missile.

As he sidled up to them, he had a lecherous smile on his face. Eric moved a step closer to Selena which only broadened Wilhelm's smile.

The German banker stared at Selena and practically drooled. "I flew into the States this week to taste this wonderful wine I've been hearing about. Now that I meet such a beautiful woman at the end of my journey, all the airport harassment and jet lag is worth the trip, even if the wine tastes of vinegar. If I may introduce myself," he held out his hand, "I am Wilhelm Schmidt."

"Selena Ramirez." She placed her hand in his and he raised it to his lips. Eric clenched his fists to keep from punching out one of his most influential guests.

The gaggle of women reminded him that he had no right. Selena was a free agent.

But his need to protect her from playboys like Wilhelm threatened to override his good sense.

"How do you know this reprobate?" Wilhelm asked her as he nodded to Eric.

"He's my boss's—"

Eric cut her off. "Reprobate?"

"Yes, we are two of a kind, are we not?" Wilhelm gestured with his wine glass as the women watched this verbal tennis match with avid interest. "So we recognize each other."

Eric took a deep breath. Wilhelm was right. But Selena knew what Eric was, so she would recognize the same in Wilhelm and not take anything he said seriously, right?

She, though, seemed to enjoy Wilhelm's overdone European manners instead of seeing through them. She smiled big and sent Eric a sparkling glance full of giggles.

Finally, after what seemed like years, she reclaimed her hand from Wilhelm. "I'm sure that

Eric's Chardonnay will make every second of your trip well worth your time."

"Madam, you are both stunning and brilliant." He toasted her, making her giggle again.

Absurdly, Eric wished he was the only one Selena giggled for. While he wished her all the happiness in the world, selfishly he wanted that happiness to stem from him.

One of the women put her manicured hand on his shoulder to claim his attention. "Eric, darling, do you think you could find me a refill?"

He shrugged off her hand, realizing he wasn't quite sure who she was. All he knew was that she wasn't Selena.

The band's segue into Bali Ha'i from *South Pacific* cued him to his grandmother's arrival. No cane or walker for her today. She arrived on the arms of two of the young servers, both dressed in tuxedoes from the twenties for their escort duties.

Before he even thought about his actions, Eric wrapped his arm around her waist and pulled her close. Selena stiffened but she didn't pull away. "I need to introduce my date to my grandmother. If you'll excuse us, Wilhelm.... Maybe you can help out—" he gestured to the woman with the red nails as the sweet desire in her eyes turn sour. Usually that would bother him, but tonight he shrugged it away.

As he guided Selena past a wine-loving Cannes-winning movie producer and his devoted lifetime partner enjoying the view at the railing, Eric considered that his abruptness with Wilhelm had bordered on insult. But the caveman in him had overruled the salesman and he just didn't care.

Selena broke into his brooding. "Wilhelm seemed pleasant. Is it true he flew all this way for tonight's uncorking?"

"Yeah, probably. He's very proud of his collection of wines from the boutique vineyards around Sonoma and Napa."

He took a glass of Pinot Gris from a passing tray and abused it by drinking it down without the proper ceremony and respect. Hell, it was his wine. He could do whatever he wanted with it. But all the time and heart that went into each vintage had him taking a mental step back to savor the fruits of his estate's labor. Over the rim, he saw his vintner, Hal, salute him and he returned the honor, before refocusing his attention on his grandmother's grand entrance.

His grandmother wore a pale blue dress and a big hat that looked like she had stolen it from the prop room of *The Great Gatsby*. Knowing her, she probably had.

With her two young men on either side, the trio walked in synchronized steps to the open patio doors where she stood until she had everyone's attention. Of course, this took only moments, since every waiter and every person associated with Walking Hill Estates knew the drill.

They all ceased their conversations and turned in his grandmother's direction. She graced everyone with her brilliant smile, the one that had earned her enough bit parts to buy this place and make a home for Eric's father and for Eric.

"We of Walking Hill are delighted to share our home and our wine with you. Welcome." Her voice carried without the slightest old-age quiver.

She gave her two gentlemen a regal nod and they each presented arms in unison. The trio made a slow and elegant processional to her rattan fan-backed chair. It had been re-cushioned to match her dress and boughs of grapevines and greenery had been draped to frame the expansive back.

The dear woman certainly knew how to set a stage. How many hours had she required the men to practice their choreography?

Once she was settled, she promptly dismissed them with a smile reminiscent of her coquettish days.

"Isn't she magnificent?" Selena whispered.

"Yes, she is." He threaded his fingers through Selena's. "As a joke, my mother taught me to call her Grandmumsy. Turns out, she thought it had a certain panache, so I still call her that."

"It fits."

"Grandmumsy *does* love a taste of the theatrical now and then."

"She does it with great flair."

"Yes. But she's not always into such pomp and circumstance. My mom spent a lot of time in theater when I was young, so Grandmumsy was the woman who held my hand when I learned to walk, colored with me when I had the measles and taught me the finer points of equestrianism. She doesn't mind hugging a mud-covered little boy whether she's wearing Ralph Lauren jodhpurs or Dickies overalls."

Why had he done that? Why had he said so much when he never, ever talked about his childhood?

Why did he want Selena to understand something more about his grandmother beyond her dramatic presentation? But, even more, why did he want Selena to understand something more about him?

He had to get a tighter grip on himself. Selena wasn't of his world. Not like those women who circled him, flattered him, and pouted when he didn't chose them.

Selena didn't want to be his chosen one.

Why didn't he want what was so easily available tonight instead of what he couldn't have?

With an imperious waggle of her finger, his grandmother motioned him to her side.

Playing the gallant, he extended his elbow to Selena. "May I present you to our matriarch?"

From the corner of his eye, he saw his grandmother nod in approval.

"I would be delighted." Selena did look pleased and maybe a touch fascinated.

Eric let out a pent up breath. Grandmumsy's regal airs had raised hackles in some of his past acquaintances.

But Selena accepting his grandmother for who she was made him feel—made him feel like he had no right to feel.

These two women would probably never meet again. So why did this moment matter so much?

Up close, Selena could see traces of Eric in his grandmother's face. The way one corner of her mouth lifted ever so slightly higher than the other corner, the stubborn chin and the kindness in her eyes were features she had passed down to her grandson.

Selena had never heard him speak of anyone with as much respect and awe as he did of the flamboyant woman in the chair in front of them. The man who laughed at life actually took his grandiose grandmother seriously.

"Grandmumsy, may I present Miss Selena Rivers." Pure love coated his introduction.

In this surreal fairy tale setting, Selena had the strangest urge to curtsey. "You have a lovely home."

"Thank you. And you are a lovely child. You may call me Mattie if you like." She held out a shaky, but well-manicured hand. Her touch was warm and firm. "Eric is a very lucky man to have such a lovely young woman in attendance tonight."

"Absolutely, Grandmumsy." He raised his grandmother's hand to his lips. "Blair sends her best."

With their gracious welcome, Selena had almost willed herself to forget that she had been a last minute replacement for Blair.

Eric's wine taster tapped him on the shoulder and spoke too softly to be overheard. Eric frowned as his eyes turned dark. Selena wanted to run her fingertips over his brows and smooth them out. Wanted to run her tongue over his lips and open them up. Wanted to take the worry from his eyes. Instead, she clasped her hands together and complimented Grandmumsy's choice of escort attire.

Eric turned toward Selena. "I've got a situation to take care of. Please excuse me."

"Of course." She wanted to assure him that she would be fine, but he had no reason to be concerned about her, did he? That would make this a real date. Or something more.

And it wasn't. She was Blair's stand-in, just doing her job, the same as when she stood in for Blair's fittings.

She took pride in doing her job well, she reminded herself as he watched Eric walk away.

She didn't need a man. She didn't need anyone. Where had that come from? Selena washed away the anger—the fear?—with a gulp of wine, then had to brace herself by putting her arm on the bulging bicep of one of the escorts.

The man gave her wink as he patted her hand. "Some men can make your world spin faster than the laws of physics, can't they?"

"It's not like that." Her protest sounded soft and fuzzy around the edges, which was exactly how the man's kind face looked too.

He lifted an eyebrow, challenging her, and she dropped her own gaze. Awkwardly, she shifted as her brain tried to develop a plan of action. Before she could, Grandmumsy leaned forward to capture her attention.

"I hope you enjoy our little tête-à-tête, my dear. Be sure to have Eric take you on the tour of the grounds. He loves this land as much as I do." Mattie took a sip of water, graciously dismissing her to greet the guests waiting patiently to pay homage to the Grande Dame of Sonoma Valley.

Resisting the urge to curtsy, Selena took off for the one place she could stand without looking too conspicuous. The bar.

As she held her glass out for a refill, she spotted Wilhelm making his way toward her. Grateful didn't begin to describe how she felt as she welcomed him with her brightest smile.

"Abandoned so soon, my dear?" As close as he leaned in to her, his breath whispered on her bare neck.

She shivered. "Eric is very in demand."

"He's a fool for leaving your side."

She pulled her attention from Eric, not even realizing she'd been staring, and gave Wilhelm her attention. His intense gaze made him seem sincere. But then, she'd seen that equally intense stare on her ex-boyfriend's cat as it stalked a lizard. Just in case Wilhelm was for real, Selena bit her lip to keep from laughing out loud at his outrageous flirtation.

Instead, she fell back on the flirting she'd practiced with Eric and gave him a dimpled smile. "And you, sir, are a gallant man."

With Eric, the flirting felt fun and made her smile as much on the inside as on the outside. With Wilhelm, it made her feel fake and uncomfortable.

Finding Eric in the crowd was easy. Instinctively, she always knew where he was.

While it was uncanny, it was also comforting. If she really needed him, she had no doubt—. But maybe she should doubt. What gave her the right to assume he'd rescue her if she needed it?

Eric mixed and mingled, but kept giving her concerned looks from across the room. She preferred to think that he was worried about her feeling awkward, rather than about her doing anything inappropriate.

Stop it, Selena! She stomped down the old, inadequate soundtrack burned into her psyche. Eric has never said or done anything to make you think he doesn't find you capable of mingling with the rich and famous.

Wilhelm wrapped his hand around hers, despite the wine glass she clutched. He was one of those men who would age gracefully, trim and silvering at the temples. That he was ten years her senior meant nothing to him.

He patted their joined hands with his free hand, bent down and looked sincerely into her eyes. "Are you all right, my dear?"

"I'm fine."

"Would you like to get away from the crowd for a bit?" His gaze shifted from her eyes to her cleavage.

She thought hard about it. He seemed to be a nice guy and being outrageously rich never hurt.

Then she felt Eric's gaze on her.

Her mouth went dry just looking at him. She took another sip of her wine.

She patted Wilhelm's hand in return then took a step back. "No, Wilhelm. Tonight I'm here for Eric."

"Should you change your mind...." He reached into his pocket and pulled out a card. His cell phone number was already handwritten on the back. He reached for her hand and tried to unfold her clenched fist.

"No." She glared at him until he put the card back into his pocket. She had never found *cheesy* to be an endearing trait. Mentally, she scratched *nice* off his description list.

Still, there had been a time.... Anything to be held close, just for a little while.

But she was past those caught-in-the-bushes days. Her next encounter would be a relationship builder, not a grins, gropes and regrets party.

The night she'd had to accept couch space and sympathetic eyes from her ex's new girlfriend, Selena had promised herself better. She had a right to expect the same deep and meaningful relationship she was willing to give. Though, sometimes she had her doubts that she would ever be at the right place at the right time.

She caught a glimpse of Eric standing between two of the women, who hadn't bothered to introduce themselves to her, as they laughed at something witty he'd said.

Not only wrong place, wrong time, but wrong desire, wrong man. Like mother, like daughter everyone used to say. She was determined to prove them wrong.

Damn, she was getting maudlin. She needed to slow down on the vino.

At an unseen signal, the waiters began exchanging wine glasses for icy water goblets. Wilhelm caught the attention of the producer holding court in a happy circle, bowed his leave of her, and moved away toward the laughter, gracefully saving face for himself.

Eric brushed into him, shoulder against shoulder, as he threaded his way toward Selena. Selena noticed that neither man apologized. She also noticed the squareness of Eric's chin, the broad fit of his shirt across his shoulders and the butt-hugging fit of his pants.

She refused to notice the way her pulse quickened and her senses heightened. She did *not* play where she worked—especially when the toy was already so well used.

She'd bet her last dollar that money didn't make playing around any more fun in the morning when she would still wake up alone.

She walked toward the patio railing and looked out over the fields. Although the sun was still up, the moon had also risen, big and round and white.

Eric snagged a goblet for her and one for himself. By the weight and cut, Selena would bet a month's pay that the glassware was crystal. Eric stood next to her, so close their elbows bumped. He rested his fingers on her bare back.

"Enjoying yourself?" His voice rumbled, low and deep and intimately close to her ear.

Is that the tone he used after sex? *Stop it, Selena. Just stop it.*

After taking a sip of water then swallowing hard, she managed to choke out, "Yes," as he waited for her to answer.

Selena took a breath that was too jagged to call calming but it helped clear her head the tiniest bit. It must be the full moon. Of course, the countless glasses of wine didn't help.

She made an effort to concentrate on what he was saying while he explained that the water would clear delicate sommelier palates.

She tried to think of something intelligent to add. "There are so many different colors in such a small area."

"We've got quite a lot of growing conditions in our four-hundred and eighty acres. Each grape variety is planted in the terroir that suits them best for flavor as well as for hardiness."

She'd never heard that proud, possessive tone in his voice before. His eyes sparkled when he talked of his land and she wanted to keep him talking.

She took another sip of water. "What's terroir?"

"The closest I can come to it is micro-climate. But it's more than that. Terroir is the feel of the land when you crumble it in your hand, the way the rains soak in or run off, the drift of the air as it heats under the sun. Terroir is more than just the sum of its parts. It's the heart and soul of the elements working together so we thrive. And, sometimes, we hit sweet ecstasy."

Talking about his land brought out the poet in him, a side she had glimpsed but had never stopped to enjoy. She had the strongest urge to lean back into him, to feel him pressed against her. As if he read her mind, he shifted forward, almost brushing her back to front then pointed with his arm rubbing against hers.

Every nerve ending in her body started popping and snapping. Her pulse sped up. She had to concentrate to suck in breath.

She gave into temptation, leaning back against him.

And the world didn't explode, although she thought, as hard as her pulse was pounding, her heart might.

"Cold?" He rubbed his arms up and down hers.

"Hmmmm," she mumbled. What was she doing?

"See that empty patch of land, the one with the fence around it." Eric spoke as if holding her was an everyday affair. But, then, they'd shared casual touches before. Maybe not quite as tender as this one, but then again maybe her interpretation was all in her head.

She forced herself to answer easily, "Yes, the one up the slope of that hill."

He shifted, proving this could definitely be more than an inconsequential instance between friends. "There's a picnic spot there and an arbor. I'd like to show it to you some day." His whisper was intimate and private. And wrong.

They were both caught up in the moment. She was flattered and so very tempted. It would be so easy. So easy to nod yes, so easy to snuggle back against him, giving him the encouragement to say more. So easy to not feel so alone tonight.

But there was her promise to herself.

And, of course, Blair.

She took a step away and they were back to being friends—except for that brittle, crackling she felt between them. "I see plenty of forests and hills unplanted. And a vegetable garden? Or are those flowers?"

He straightened and shifted back, too. "We only farm about a fifth right now. The stables, arena barn and house and table garden take up a few acres. We're experimenting with the effect of different floral combinations with some of our vegetables. Our chef is having a great time adding wild bergamot and pansies to our salads and watching some of the older hands try them for the first time." His tone was so stiff, he could have been reading from a public relations brochure.

Good, Selena, good. Keep it friendly but impersonal. "Does the staff live on the estate?"

"We offer that option. Our chef lives on the grounds. So does our viticulturist and our winemaker. We've got a little community over that rise." He pointed toward a hill that had crops growing up the side in neat rows as if they defied gravity. "We call that planting of Chardonnay grapes up there, Mattie's Melody. Those are the grapes that yielded our Select wine that we're presenting tonight. We've been experimenting with different varietals for that particular soil type for a while now and, with the weather just right, we hit pay dirt this year."

His tone and his words were so correct that Selena found herself questioning if she had misinterpreted his intent earlier. Had the wine colored her hearing? The vino certainly had her mixing metaphors. Was it too big a step to think that she had infused his platonic offer with more subtle intent? He had only offered a picnic, after all. And he hadn't mentioned anything about just the two of them.

She took a big gulp of water. "It's amazing to think all this has happened within the last century."

"Within the last few years, actually. The estate was more of a hobby for my grandmother when she bought it and my dad wasn't really interested in farming. But the science and the magic of it all fascinates me." He pointed into a thickly wooded area, not touching her at all. "We just finished adding onto the winery to expand the storage for the red wines."

Selena squinted to make out the subtle architecture of the wood-sided buildings set among the trees. They blended with the natural beauty of their surroundings. "Will we get to see the winery?"

"I don't let the public in there. But I'd love to give you a private showing." His deep voice reached down and tickled low in her belly, despite her best efforts to ignore how horny she was. Damned full moon.

She could walk away. She could run.

They stood in silence. Selena was aware of every flicker of Eric's eyelashes when he blinked. His breaths fell into rhythm with hers, a slow, full, in-and-out that should have felt comfortable, not visceral and profound.

No, this couldn't be happening. She couldn't be falling for Eric. She had a job she loved. A job that would fall apart the second Eric's lust turned to boredom.

Selena attempted to go over her to-do list in her head, but found herself loosing track. She had never noticed that Eric smelled so good, like soap and water and sunshine.

Behind them, conversation settled into a quiet mumble punctuated only by an occasional laugh or clink of glassware being collected by the staff.

Although the sun wouldn't set for another hour and a half, the air grew chill. Eric ran his hand across her shoulder and down her arm. Her skin prickled, but she couldn't attribute her response solely to the external temperature. In fact, her internal temperature shot up several degrees.

She must remember Blair. Being enfolded in Eric's embrace was not Selena's rightful place. She was a personal assistant, a stand-in, and nothing else. She crossed her arms and took a step away.

Eric looked over and cocked an eyebrow at the pink-suited woman. Apparently that was mogul speak for, *get my guest her wrap,* because the woman left the patio then return with Selena's shawl. "Thanks."

He took the Pashmina and draped it over Selena's shoulders.

Eric stood behind her so closely that she could feel the heat he radiated.

Or maybe it was her in heat. Her judgment was shot and her imagination was running wild.

So maybe this was a castle. But there was no horse-drawn carriage, no fairy godmother. Even if Eric would make an awesome prince, she was no Cinderella. And there was no such thing as happily-ever-after. She forced herself to think of practicalities.

Of course, Eric had to stand close to help her with her shawl. How silly would he have been had he just tossed the shawl in her general direction? And it had been only a flight of fancy that she imagined his hands lingering as he smoothed and arranged.

"Better?" His voice sent delicious shivers along her arms.

She didn't have to feel guilty about her fantasies, did she? She didn't mean to act on them, did she? Who had to know? And fighting them wasn't working.

She let her feelings flow. Was this better?

"Yes. Much."

He took a step back and cold air rushed between them. "I'm so sorry to abandon you for the next few minutes but I've got to check on the tour arrangements."

At least she had had a few moments of pretended bliss. Even fantasies couldn't last forever.

CHAPTER FIVE

The crystal tap on a water goblet drew the attention of Selena as well as everyone else on the patio.

Mattie held her glass high. "Walking Hill Estate would like to offer you a view into our past, our future, our toil and our dreams. We now invite you to explore our vineyards to offer greater insight into the fruits of our labors. We've arranged carriage rides around our grounds that we hope you will enjoy."

As everyone paired off, Selena took a look around for Eric. When she couldn't find him, she looked for anyone who would give her a welcoming glance and let them join their party.

No one.

She stared down into her glass, twisting it and watching the wine grow tears as it dripped down the bowl.

"Selena?" Wilhelm's voice behind her made her jump.

She looked up, surprised to see his worry in his eyes as he looked at her from under his lashes. Without his flirtatious confidence, he looked shy and boyish and as awkward as she felt.

"Yes?"

"I sometimes come across stronger than I mean to. It's just that socializing is difficult for me. I never seem to find the right balance. I'm sorry to have offended you."

Selena knew how that felt. Eric had her so off-balance he was making her dizzy. "Apology accepted."

"If you tell me to go, I will bother you no longer but I was hoping—" He swallowed, took a breath and then finished. "If you would give me another chance. I would really like to get to know you better."

He smiled with the kind of anxious grimace that revealed he was shy, maybe even terrified. Even though his bank balance must increase by a half-million a week, riches hadn't erased his fear of rejection.

Again and again, Selena learned that Mom was wrong on that lesson. Money didn't cure everything.

His fingers tightened into a white-knuckled clench around the stem of his wine glass.

It should have been easy. Wilhelm had gone too far, too fast.

But now, his vulnerability touched her. He even fidgeted while he gazed past her shoulder, waiting for her answer. While Selena had never been shy, she'd certainly had her fair share of rejection.

To stall, she took a sip of the wine she had vowed to slow down on. She scanned the room, knowing her hedging tactics weren't as discreet as they should be. Were there no other unattached women here? Selena did a fast glance around the room, realizing that at least a half dozen men milled around, unattached.

Where the hell was Eric? She was supposed to be here for him, right?

She gave herself a mental shake.

Apparently, she and Eric weren't giving off 'we're a couple' vibes. But then, why should they? They weren't a couple. She was his date. No, not even that. She was his stand-in for Blair. Nothing but a warm body to keep the numbers at the table even. What was the protocol here?

At the moment, Wilhelm had the friendliest face in the crowd and Eric was nowhere in sight. She had to admit that she enjoyed the admiration in his eyes as he looked at her. And it wouldn't hurt to put her attraction to Eric into perspective.

"That's very kind of you, Wilhelm."

"Not kind at all. My pleasure."

"I would be delighted." She touched her fingertips to his sleeve and gave him the friendliest smile she had in her.

He extended his arm, accidentally bumping his elbow into her breast. If he hadn't reddened she might have thought he'd done it on purpose, but his blush proved he hadn't.

"Sorry." His mumble barely reached her ears.

She took his arm careful not to lean toward him. "No problem." While she wouldn't go so far as to say that he felt nice and comfortable like someone she could easily have as a guy-pal, he kept her from feeling like an extraneous tagalong.

Following Walking Hill's staff, the guests grouped together and headed for the stairs leading down below the patio.

Horse-drawn surreys lined the pathway.

She gaped and stumbled. Oh, shit. Was that a costumed fairy godmother twinkling in the bushes?

Wilhelm caught her arm. "You okay?"

She clung to him a little longer than she should have. "Just hunky-dory."

Eric came through the house onto the patio and saw her on Wilhelm's arm. He quirked an eyebrow, then made a ninety degree turn to speak with his winemaker, Ricky.

In unison, the men turned and waded into the crowd.

"Wilhelm," Ricky said as soon as he was in hearing distance, "I had hoped you would ride with me."

"And I'll be glad to escort Selena. After all, she is *my* date for the evening." Eric held his hand out to Selena as if he expected her to follow his bidding.

She felt Wilhelm stiffen, although his demeanor never changed. She knew how it felt to be abandoned at the whim of others and she took a subtle step closer to him.

Ricky said, "I have some points of interest I would like to discuss with you about our new Cabernet project. We want to model the air patterns and heat effects but don't know which software would be easiest to use." He sweetened the pot as if Wilhelm could be so obviously bribed away.

Selena tightened her grip on Wilhelm's arm, but he was already prying her fingers loose. "Sure. I know exactly what you need. It would take a bit of modification, though." Wilhelm's eyes wore a happy glaze as if he saw Nirvana in the distance.

Apparently, he didn't mind dumping her for Walking Hill's winemaker.

His quick abandonment was a not-so-subtle reminder that Selena was a terrible judge of men.

Eric graciously put his arm around her shoulders and squeezed. She sighed. Nothing like a brotherly hug to soothe the pain.

As Wilhelm and Ricky rejoined the queue, she overheard Wilhelm use the same cajoling tone of voice he'd used with her when he said, "I'd consider it a personal favor if you would...

Ricky nodded yes, but Selena didn't hear the rest of his answer because Eric choose that moment to whisper in her ear, "I hope you don't mind, but Wilhelm can be such a lecher. Besides, it *is* my party. It seems only fair that I get to pick my partner."

She was already feeling buzzed from the wine. His whisper went straight to her head—and other softer places. "Maybe I was looking forward to being leched."

"Leched? Is that a real word?" His laugh was short and on the tense side.

When she didn't laugh back, he said, "You're not serious, are you?"

"It's been a while." How many months had it been since she had last flirted, much less anything more? A woman needed a good ego- boost every now and then.

Selena watched as Ned waved his hands animatedly toward a hillside of grapevines. "But then, it seems Wilhelm finds Ricky a superior replacement for me."

"You," he ran a forefinger along her jaw line, "cannot be replaced."

She looked into his eyes and found the most fascinating shades of blue and gray along with a generous spark of warmth. With the smallest tweak of her imagination, she could imagine that the warmth was heat for her. Her fantasy soothed her ego nicely.

The sound of horses' hooves clopping down below brought her out of her trance-like exploration. "They're leaving us behind."

"It's okay. I know my way around."

He led her down the stair and seated her in the two-person surrey, as the last of the four seated buggies pulled away.

Serena batted at the pom-pom fringe around the roof. "It's like a scene out of *Oklahoma*."

"That's exactly were the buggies came from. Mattie enjoys studio prop auctions."

"I thought she might." Serena knew she should hold herself apart from Eric, but with the wine and the horses and the beginnings of stars twinkling overhead, she couldn't keep herself from relaxing. The rhythm of the ride was so seductive. With each sway, Eric's thigh rubbed against the length of hers sending pulses of energy straight to her solar plexus.

She leaned in closer as they moved into the cooler shadows. Eric shifted toward her, too. His scent was so distinctive. Fresh air and soap and masculinity.

Her sense of smell always became highly sensitive when her pheromones went on overdrive. She *could* blame her hyper-awareness on the wine, but a little private fantasizing never hurt anyone, did it?

Eric leaned toward her. "That big buggy in the lead was in *The Wizard of Oz*."

This *was* turning into the most surreal fairy-tale she could have ever dreamed about. Maybe there was a fairy godmother in the bushes! Maybe this was Selena's very own dream-come-true.

She needed to say something, anything, to keep the spell going. "And the horses?"

"Our little mare belongs to the Estate. The larger horses are Percherons. They're stabled here, but they belong to our chef who trains them as a hobby."

Eric gave a firm voice command to the impatient mare and loosened the reins, allowing her to step lively.

The pink-suited woman in the lead buggy began speaking via a small speaker on the floorboard about the vineyard.

Selena sighed with relief when she realized she wouldn't have to keep her end of the conversation going. She intended to sit back and enjoy the sensations, at least until her head cleared.

Time passed in a delightful haze. Vaguely, she heard the speaker drone on about vertical planting methods and bringing a vineyard from cuttings to fruition in five years for a modest yield, and ten to get it right. *Ten years!*

Her personal philosophy was to look only ten minutes down that futuristic road. That way, you couldn't build up pipedreams, only to have them blown away on a capricious ill wind. And, right now she was experiencing a spectacular ten minutes.

She and Eric had spent many quiet hours in each other's company, but now she felt different. She felt at peace. Even the increased sensual awareness fed into her sense of wholeness, her contentment that her universe was just as it should be.

The stillness of the buggy alerted her that they had stopped. Around her, guests were climbing from their buggies, laughing and chattering.

She looked over to find that he was looking down at her. She blinked herself back to reality and cleared her throat. "I guess I wasn't such a good conversationalist. Thank you for putting up with my poor company."

"You were excellent company. You always are."

She could drown in his deep voice.

Come on, Selena. Let's work through the buzz, here. You've got another bout of sipping and a supper to get through. She sat up and rubbed her hands down her arms to stimulate circulation. "And you, sir, always know the right thing to say."

Eric looked as if he might say more, but then he stopped himself and climbed from the surrey. He held up his hand to her. When she reached for it he grabbed her around the waist and lifted her down instead. His move made her feel so feminine, so cherished. She felt safe.

"Thanks. She looked up into his eyes and swayed as if she were spellbound.

His hands tightened on her waist. "Are you steady, there?"

"Yes, I'm fine. Just a bit light-headed."

Eric held onto her as they climbed the steps back up to the patio. Her focus was dreamy and the most subtle of smiles played on her mouth. He let himself take credit for that soft look on her face, even though reality whispered that it was most likely the wine.

He slid his hand from her arm to her back and let it rest there. Her body radiated heat even through her shawl. He was trying to think of something to say, something low and quiet so that she would have to lean into him to hear when one of his grandmother's pretty boys presented himself to her.

"Pardon me, Miss Selena, but Miss Mattie would like to extend an invitation to sit next to her during supper."

Without thought, Eric pulled Selena closer to him. She had to put one hand between them to push away. "I would be delighted." With a quick wink at Eric, she left with the server.

Eric had a hard time concentrating on what that wink might mean as he watched her beautiful backside walk away.

Ricky sought him out, noticed the direction of Eric's attention and joined him in the perusal. "Taken in parts she's not that pretty, but when she listens to you talk, she just sparkles."

Not that pretty? She's the most stunning woman I've ever seen. Eric almost said it aloud, but stopped himself before he pointed out Ricky's lunacy.

Women liked Ricky. He was always with a tall emaciated model or starlet. But what if Ricky realized the error of his ways and started to prefer someone more like Selena? Eric would hate to have to pull rank on the best winemaker in the valley. It could result in a much worse problem than sour grapes.

Eric stopped himself right there. He had no right to keep Selena away from anyone. But his protective urges said otherwise. She deserved better than a love 'em and leave 'em type.

She deserved better than him.

She nodded, taking his excuse at face value.

When Eric arrived at the table, he applauded the grace and intelligence of his grandmother. She had maneuvered the seating arrangements so that Selena sat closest to him in a place of honor previously reserved for her. Mattie could be quite a matchmaker when she set her mind to it. Apparently, after meeting Selena, she had set her mind to it.

He would have to set her straight later.

But for now—for now, what would it hurt to go with it and enjoy himself for just a few short hours.

Mattie sat two chairs down, on Selena's other side. As he passed behind her, he kissed his grandmother on her cheek. "Thank you."

He would have kissed Selena, too, but knew he couldn't have stopped at her cheek, not when he could stand over her shoulder and admire the deep valley of cleavage. No other man better try to stand behind her this evening.

As the Chardonnay was uncorked and allowed to breathe, Walking Hill's expert tasting panel made speeches about dedication and luck, about science and magic and about their love of the land. Every speech was made with passion and sincerity. Eric's heart swelled as they all confirmed their passions for stewardship and nurturing and for being a part of Walking Hill. Selena watched each speaker, her attention focused on them.

Underneath the table, her hand sought out his and squeezed.

She knew. She understood that this was one of the most important nights of his life. His heart swelled, as she witnessed the honor being given to his life's work.

As the Sonoma Valley Wine Association's president took the opportunity to promote Sonoma Wine in general, Eric let his thoughts wander. While he would have never wished hives on Blair, he thanked the fates for intervening and setting his world on the proper path. Now he would do his part to make sure that he and Selena continued on course to become more than just friends.

A server poured for Selena and Eric watched, eagle-eyed, to make sure the man's attention stayed on Selena's glass.

Was this jealousy? He'd never experienced it before over a woman. Even his ex-wife had never stirred these caveman-like feelings in him. He shifted in his chair, discreetly trying to find a comfortable position.

The servers poured and everyone around the table raised a glass to inspect Walking Hill's finest. A frown creased Selena's brow as she followed Mattie's lead to the nth degree.

He had the strongest urge to whisper to her that form and function didn't matter. What mattered was that she was by his side.

He had a quick mental image of sipping wine from her bellybutton. His private party would be a blanket, an arbor and an open sky with their clothes scattered around them.

The silence of the room brought him back to reality. He needed to stand and make the first sip but standing wasn't such a great idea at the moment.

He made a great show of rolling the wine in his glass, then sniffing the bouquet, while he used a ploy he hadn't had to use since high school. Silently, he recited Edgar Allen Poe's grim poem, The Raven. He finished the first stanza and found he needed to go on to the second one. By the time the last 'nevermore' came around, he was ready.

He stood and raised his glass to his grandmother. "To the woman whose vision has now become reality." Then he took a sip, held it on his tongue, swished and swallowed.

The bouquet, the taste, the afternotes were all perfect. He saluted his guests and they all followed his ritual.

Applause broke out. Not quiet-opera or golf-tournament-type applause, but genuine, enthusiastic hand clapping. He asked his tasting panel to stand and the applause renewed itself. From the glint in each sommelier's eyes, Eric could tell that this year's Select Chardonnay would be sold out by the end of the evening.

As the guests finished their glasses, baskets of light flaky croissants arrived along with plates of salad. He shook his head at the artistic creation the servers put down in front of him. Even knowing he would be expected to munch on the edible flowers intermixed with the delicate greens couldn't put a damper on this moment.

Selena ate her salad with the same enthusiasm she did everything else. As he picked around a pansy, he saw her chomp down on a piece of cactus without hesitation.

The quail and fruit compote that followed were easier to swallow. In fact, they were delicious. By the happy buzz around the room, Eric could tell that his guests were enjoying the whole experience, too. On his right, Mattie kept Selena involved in conversation. Clearly, the change of seating arrangements wasn't for his benefit alone. Instead, Mattie used her time to scope out Selena, asking questions like, "Where is that delightful accent from?" and "Would you tell me about your first meeting with my grandson?"

As brilliant as Selena was, he had no doubt that she understood Mattie's motives. The happy sound of her voice reassured him that she didn't seem to mind. In fact, she seemed to be enjoying herself without his conversation.

He had always admired Selena's independence, but, right now, he wouldn't mind helping her out, saving her from his grandmother's nosiness. Being the sole object of her attention instead of being ignored. He'd never had to work to keep a woman's attention before.

But then, Selena only saw him as Blair's sidekick, didn't she?

His ego stung—a lot.

On his left, Ricky answered Wilhelm's multitude of questions so he was left with nothing to do but brood.

Finally, Mattie signaled for her young men and they came forward to help her from her chair. She stood and made a graceful gesture toward the glass doors. "It's a beautiful night for music. Please join us on the patio, and feel free to dance if the mood strikes you."

The sun had fully set and the patio glistened with hundreds of candles in hurricane lamps. Twinkling lights had been wound through the railings while they were touring. The full moon and stars overhead cast wispy shadows on the flagstone.

Strains of Shall We Dance from *The King and I* filled the evening.

How rude would it be to leave his guests, throw Selena over his shoulder and whisk her off to that arbor? His fantasy included Selena unbuttoning his shirt as they strode away from the crowd.

As the guests filed out, Mattie put her hand on Selena's shoulder. "My dear, I'm afraid I will have to forgo the dancing tonight. Would you take the first dance with my grandson?"

She looked past Selena and arched her eyebrow at Eric.

First dance? Eric never danced. He hated to dance. His grandmother knew that. The sooner he could explain that her matchmaker efforts were being wasted, the easier this would be for all of them.

Being the delightful escort Selena was, she dimpled and said, "I would be delighted to."

He would be so outclassed. She was already swaying to the music as she sat in her chair.

"Let's go with the box-step, all right?" He didn't add that he only knew that much because Mattie had insisted on his learning the social graces as a trade-off when he'd wanted to take martial arts at eight years old. He'd stuck with the martial arts but been allowed to drop those painful dance lessons at twelve.

Eric held Selena's chair for her, taking the opportunity to *accidentally* run his hand along her bare back. When she didn't flinch or pull away, he took it as a good sign. Very deliberately, he placed his palm on her lower back to guide her to the patio. Again, no stiffening or moving away.

He owed his grandmother an apology for resisting all those lessons. Dancing might have some merit after all.

With Mattie regally ensconced in her chair, Eric held out his hand to Selena to lead her onto the cleared portion of the patio.

She wrapped her arms around him and whispered, "I'm not too good at this, so nothing fancy, please. And you'll have to hold me close so I can follow, okay?" Her breath was warm on his neck.

"Of course. Whatever you need." Her body heat made his blood boil.

Oh, yeah. He just might learn to love dancing after all. "You'll be wonderful. Just relax and watch my eyes."

He had no idea what the eye-watching thing was really about, but it was coming in handy right now.

After the first step or two, Selena became pliant under his guiding hand. That she followed where he led really got him off.

"Having a good time?" He swept her around another couple.

"I feel like a princess in a fairy tale being swept off her feet by the handsome prince." She giggled and pulled him tighter.

Eric bobbled a step and did a sweeping turn to cover.

Selena usually delivered those kinds of snippets coated in a thick layer of teasing. Her voice had never held that sincere tone before.

Or was he just wanting to hear more than was really there. And she'd had quite a bit to drink, too.

Regardless, Eric felt rather like a white knight as he stopped counting steps and simply swayed from side to side, holding Selena tight.

Selena was abnormally quiet after that. Eric didn't want to break the spell.

Wilhelm broke it for them. "Forgive the intrusion, but I would like to cut in if the gracious lady would allow."

That's it. Wilhelm was off the guest list, regardless of how many cases of Select he usually purchased.

Say no. Say no, he thought at Selena. Sometimes, he could swear they read each other's minds. Let tonight be one of those times.

Selena could see Eric wanting her to refuse Wilhelm as clearly as if he said the words out loud. But why? And why hadn't he laughed when she said the thing about being a princess. Yes, she'd meant it. But she hadn't meant for *him* to know she meant it.

And now he didn't want her to dance with Wilhelm? Why?

Whatever his reasons, she was sure hers overrode his.

She was confused. And wanting. And totally out of her element.

And she wanted to go home.

But more than that, she wanted Eric to keep holding her tight. To let his hands roam down her back. To plant shivering kisses down her neck and along her shoulders.

And that's why she needed to dance with Wilhelm.

"Yes. I'll dance with you." She reached past him and took Wilhelm's extended hand. Letting go of Eric felt like letting go of her a warmth that reached so deep inside her, it was a part of her.

Selena took Wilhelm's damp, cold hand as he held her an arm's length away. At their first step, she stumbled, feeling unanchored.

He clenched her hand tighter. "So sorry."

Selena tore her attention away from Eric's backside as he walked off the dance floor and back Wilhelm. "Not at all. It was my misstep."

Wilhelm led her into a stiff, enthusiastic turn that ended up in an empty dark corner of the patio. Still dancing his heavy two- step, he said, "I must apologize for my earlier suggestion. I did not realize that you had a relationship with Eric."

Selena thought about correcting him, but decided against it. His false assumption would take care of a lot of possible problems.

"We don't—" Wait. Did Eric want Wilhelm to think they had a relationship? "It's complicated. But thank you for asking me to dance." She meant that sincerely. Each second in Eric's arms left her more and more confused.

"My pleasure." He kept dancing, but the mechanical way he moved showed that his thoughts were not on the dance. "I would like to explain so you will not think me a boorish man. Eric is usually with Blair, all very friendly and understood by those close to him. When I learned that you are Blair's assistant, here because she was ill, I thought you were only taking her place. So I did not understand. I should have been more observant. Anyone could see that it is different for you and him, than for Blair and him. Again, my most sincere apologies."

Selena didn't know how to respond. "Think nothing more of it, Wilhelm. And you will be forever forgiven if you will find me another glass of wine."

"Of course." Wilhelm bowed, just like on a black-and-white movie, and set off for the nearest tray of glasses.

Selena breathed deeply, but it didn't help clear the confusion Wilhelm's impassioned speech had caused.

As if he called her name, she felt compelled to search for Eric. He stood against the railing, alone, studying her. The moonlight sculpted his face into angles and planes. She wanted to run her fingers across his jaw and soften the hard line of his mouth. She wanted to kiss his lips and hear him whisper love words in her ear. She wanted him to hold her tight and never let her go.

She was so confused.

Eric tried to keep from glowering as he watched Selena dance. Tonight, she sparkled and he wanted to feel her magic again.

But then, she'd put her spell on him a long time ago.

At his side, his grandmother put her delicate hand on his. "She seems like a lovely young lady."

"She is."

"I want you to be happy."

Now was the time to put an end to any false hopes or expectations. "I won't date her."

"Why not?"

"She's not my type."

"You mean she's not one of those good-time girls you're usually seen with?"

"Exactly."

"Then I think she might be exactly your type."

Eric couldn't even imagine presenting Selena with a diamond necklace while he assured her it was him, not her, and then thanking her for their time together with his firm assurance she would find someone better than him soon.

Because he couldn't stop himself, he walked toward Selena and Wilhelm on the edge of the dance floor.

With little grace and even less subtlety, Eric placed himself between Selena and Wilhelm. "I believe you promised me this dance."

She didn't say no, she'd never promised him anything. Instead, she held out her arms to him letting him pull her close, letting him breathe in her scent and letting him stop thinking about shoulds and shouldn'ts, just like Blair had advised him.

He held her as they box-stepped and she followed his lead as if they had been dancing together for years.

He caught himself humming the refrain of Do I Love You Because You're Beautiful? as the band played. With anyone else he would have become embarrassed, but with Selena, he knew she wouldn't laugh at his missed notes.

Becoming daring, he swung her in a sweeping circle. She stumbled and he caught her, holding her close to his chest.

"Sorry." He mumbled into her hair. He smoothed back the pieces that had escaped to make a halo around her head in the misty light.

She caught at his wrist and squinted at the face of his watch. "Is it twelve already? Dominic is probably waiting."

"Not yet. We've got a few minutes." One of the traits he most admired in Selena was her sense of responsibility. But right now, he wished she would be just a bit more frivolous.

"He's got to get back to relieve Allan." She started walking toward the doors leading back into the house.

"I'll walk you to the car."

"But your guests-"

"-can live without me a few minutes." He snatched her hat from a patio table, followed her through the house and out the front door.

They stood on the entrance stairs and watched as a car wound its way up the driveway. When she shivered against the chill, he stood behind her and wrapped his arms around her.

She turned to him and put barely a hands-breadth between them. The vastness of the sky made her want to whisper.

"I really had a great time." Her voice sounded husky in the night air.

"I'm glad." He returned her whisper, leaning in close so she could hear him.

Selena shivered despite the warmth of her shawl as she looked to the night sky to break their connection.

"They say a full moon makes you feel crazy things."

"Do you feel crazy things, Selena?"

Her mouth went dry. She licked her lips as she nodded yes.

"Me, too." As Eric's lips came closer to hers, she was sure they were right.

Way back in her mind was who he was, who she was and what she should not do. But right before her was Eric, with dreamy eyes, full lips and hands that crept from her waist, higher to her rib cage so that his thumbs caressed the undersides of her breasts.

Her hands were doing their own roaming up his back, along his jaw line and through his hair.

She closed the gap between them, her tongue flickering out for a taste. Did that deep sigh come from her or from him? Did it matter? No. Nothing mattered but the vortex that spun faster and faster so around them so that the center of her world was Eric.

They kissed with a bond that Selena had never felt before. Their passion was fueled by their intermingled breaths, by their palms touching skin, by their heartbeats against each other's chests. Selena had never felt such desire from a kiss before.

His hands traveled along her arms, across her bare back, dipping low beneath the bodice of her sundress. Her hands pulled at his shirt, wanting, hurting for the touch of his chest and stomach against hers with a frantic need she'd never had before. She fumbled and tugged at the buttons until they came undone.

Then she reached around under his shirt, ran her hands over the small of his back, over his shoulder blades, up to his neck, pulling him closer so that his warm, bare chest pressed against her aching breasts.

Night's perfume became overshadowed by the primal scent of man wanting woman. Her mouth devoured his, trying to merge one into the other.

She wanted. God, how she wanted.

Lightning flashed, the brightness fueling her craving.

"Damn." Eric ground out against her mouth. His hands left her back, left her shoulders and intervened between her ribcage and his. He pushed at her and she resisted, not understanding. His lips left hers and she felt bereft and cold.

He took a step back. "Photographers."

What? The word made no sense to her in her world of passionate touch, feel, smell and taste.

"Selena, the photographers." His fingers shook as he buttoned up his shirt. He bent down to grab the hat and shawl she didn't remember dropping. "Let's go somewhere and finish this." His hand reached for hers.

"Selena?" Dominic's Southern accent cut through her fog. "Are you ready?"

Dominic! Blair! Blair's boyfriend, Eric! What was she doing? What was she thinking? No. No thinking to it. It was all feeling and she knew damned well what she was feeling. Pure, unadulterated lust.

Frustration, guilt and confusion flooded her senses.

She pulled her hand from his. "I've got to go."

"But..."

"Thanks, I had a good time."

"But...?"

"I have to leave now."

Eric tightened his hold on her, then forced himself to let her go.

The last notes of Some Enchanted Evening faded away.

As quickly as she could on her shaking knees, she walked down the stairs, not even bothering to leave a slipper behind.

Dominic opened her door and held out a hand to help her in. She dodged it, not wanting anyone's touch. She settled into the deep seats and wrapped her arms around herself. *You just can't leave well enough alone, can you, Selena?* With Blair, she had the perfect job, the perfect budding friendship, the perfect life. And now what?

Dominic was back to his normal reticence, so she had the whole hour and a half to brood in silence. She used her time well.

CHAPTER SIX

When Selena left, she took the life of the party with her. Eric's guests milled around for a few more minutes then began their departures, which suited Eric just fine. He had some thinking to do, after a cold shower.

Had the need in Selena's eyes, in her touch and in her mouth been equal to his?

Damn those photographers.

Or maybe he should thank them.

Nothing good could come from kissing Selena. In fact, something very, very bad might come from it instead.

Icy water dripped down his neck and spine.

Would Selena feel he'd taken advantage of her? Had he?

No, the desire had been as heavy in her eyes as it was in him.

But she'd had quite a bit to drink. Had she been caught up in the moment? Was that his excuse, too?

He dried off and slung his towel toward the laundry basket.

What should he do?

He would talk to her. Isn't that what women always wanted? To talk? Yes, that's what he would do. The sooner the better, so she wouldn't have time to think.

He would drive to Blair's. If Selena was already asleep, he'd camp out in Blair's guest room to be the first person Selena talked to in the morning. He'd make sure they could still be friends.

The thought of losing Selena as his friend made him shiver.

He pulled on a pair of jeans and a T-shirt and headed for his car.

He would fix this, reassure her that the kiss was nothing. Just moonlight madness.

Eric scrubbed his hand through his hair.

He'd never lied to Selena before. He wasn't looking forward to it now.

Blair doodled on the yellow legal pad while she waited for Dominic to come upstairs. Only one afternoon of R & R and she was already so bored she could scream.

Instead of song lyrics, her page was filled with childish drawings of hearts intertwined and happy faces.

The minute she saw Dom's expression, she asked, "What's wrong?"

"There was paparazzi at Eric's tonight."

"Yeah? So?"

"One of them got shots of Selena and Eric saying goodbye."

"And?"

"And I think it embarrassed Selena." He rubbed his hand over his face. "They were sucking face big time when he started shooting."

"No kidding? Way to go, Eric!" She pumped her fist into the air. "It's about time he made a move. I can't wait to congratulate him."

"I don't think so." He slipped off his tennis shoes. "Selena practically ran to the car and she didn't say anything all the way back."

"Oh." Blair puzzled about that one for a while. Not good. "Not even about the wine or the food, or anything?"

"Nope." He unbuttoned his shirt, distracting Blair until she remembered her plan.

"Did you eat?" Springing new ideas on Dominic always worked better when he had a full stomach.

"Yes, mother hen. I ate."

"At Merv's?"

"Am I that predictable?"

"Only to me." She doodled a big heart-shaped balloon and wrote their initials in it.

"Huh-uh." He let his shirt fall to the floor followed by his pants. "You've got that tone in your voice."

"What tone?" She tried to sound naïve and innocent.

"The one that says you're going to try to sell me on something I'm not going to like."

"I just thought that maybe..."

He climbed into bed and kicked the covers off his side onto Blair. "Maybe what, Blair?"

"You don't have to sound like you're about to say no before I even get started." She paused while she shoved the covers back to his side as she always did. Rituals were so comforting. "Maybe we could encourage them a little bit."

He put his hands behind his head and stared bleakly at the ceiling. "So that's what you've been doing. Making him play chauffeur when you got delayed at the doctor's office, making sure Selena went to the party in your place—all contrived. You're trying to match make."

"Those were just opportunities. Apparently, they need more help than that. They're made for each other, if they'd just open their eyes and see it."

"Seems to me they're not the first couple to be voluntarily blind to each other."

"But look how much happier we are now that we've stopped fighting against ourselves." Blair drew two stick figures, a girl and a boy holding hands, and labeled them Selena and Eric. "Besides, Eric's the one who finally pushed you over the edge."

"I am *not* going to deliberately try to make him jealous. That was a poor trick." Dominic blew out a deep breath. "The only reason he got to keep his face in order was because I knew that you had orchestrated the whole thing and he was only the poor dupe you talked into carrying it out."

"I just love it when you talk tough. Besides, you played that part in the tractor video a lot better than Eric ever could have."

"Right." He heaved another sigh. "What is my role in this production?"

"I'm still working on it."

The whop-whop of a helicopter beat overhead. Probing lights reflected through the veranda French doors as the helicopter swooped low over the house.

Dominic got up and closed the heavy drapes behind the sheers. "The publicity vampires are out tonight. News must be slow in Celebrityland for them to be flying all the way up to Northern California."

"My album got topped today. A cute little brunette with a really great voice took the number one album spot on Billboard and spots one and two for singles." She leaned her head against his shoulder. "Dom, I'm really worried. The new video will air in three weeks, the tour is less than two months away and the clothing line is making its debut. Without buzz, all of it could flop."

"Honey, you've got talent. You're not just a fad or a lucky break. Your career will survive this little setback. Try not to fret. Worry will only make you recover slower."

"Fret. I just adore your Southern accent." She trickled her finger across her chest. "You know that publicity makes you or breaks you. But this plan I'm working on—if Eric and Selena agree to help out, I think we can keep it from breaking us. And you'll back me up, right?"

"Back you up? Is this something they may not want to do?" He caught her wandering hand and kissed her palm. "Do you know how much I love you? Of course, you do. Otherwise you couldn't talk me into your schemes."

"I love you, too."

Dom's phone vibrated on the table. "Looks like the unsuspecting lover-boy is here."

"Great! Is he going back to Selena's cottage?" Blair vaulted out of bed and ran over to the window to peep out.

Dom squinted as he scrolled through a screen. "Nope. The heat sensors are tracking him to his guest room."

"Damn." Blair padded back to the bed and crawled under the covers.

Dom straightened them over her shoulder the way she liked them, then he reached over and turned out the light. "Stop plotting and start sleeping. You need your rest."

Blair snuggled against his side and tried to sleep but a welt on her right shoulder started to itch. She distracted herself by working out the finer details of her plans for Eric and Selena.

Tomorrow, she would roll out her plan to rock their world and hopefully keep hers rocking, too.

Selena stared at her bedside clock as the hands lined up at twelve and three. She had watched each second tick by as sleep ran further and further away.

Finally, she got up, wiggled into her swimsuit and grabbed a towel. This was the first and would probably be the last time she wore her custom-fitted one piece.

No great clothes, no job, no place to sleep, all because she had rotten self-control when it came to boy-girl attraction.

The goldenrod yellow, high cut thighs and low cut halter style cleavage made the most of her curves and coloring. At least she would look good on her way out.

She called Allan to let him know she wanted to take a swim. No sense in breaking the never-swim-alone rule just because she had broken the never-kiss-the-boss's-boyfriend rule.

"Hold on, Selena. I'll be right down."

"Thanks, Allan. I could really use the exercise."

"I know how that is."

While she waited for Allan, she dipped her toe in the water. Chilly, but it would feel fine once she took the plunge.

Allan came down carrying his monitor. He flipped on the soft lights that made the water turn from inky black to aqua blue. "Do you want the overhead lights on?"

"No. I'd rather not." She took a breath and dove. Underwater, she swam back and forth, breaking the surface only when she had to breathe.

Isolated by the water, she could pretend that she was alone in the world with nobody to answer to, nobody to apologize to and nobody to say goodbye to. She concentrated on the water surrounding her and nothing else. With each lap, she sought answers on how she could have gone so wrong and what she could do to fix it.

After twenty laps, her anaerobic capacity became exhausted before her mind did. The only answer she came up with was that she was screwed.

On spaghetti arms and legs, she crawled from the pool. At least she was tired enough to sleep now. The night air made her shiver as she wrapped a towel around her dripping hair.

She reached for her other towel, but her trembling hand dropped it.

"Let me help." Allan reached down to get the towel as a helicopter swooped in low, blasted them with a spotlight that had them wincing and then flew away.

Allan shook his head. "What kind of photo quality did they hope to get?"

It didn't matter. Tonight alone they had shots of her on Dominic's arm as she walked up Eric's mansion steps, of Eric kissing her as she left and now of Allan with his arms around her. She was paying for some bad karma, but why all in one night? She hugged her towel around her.

As she blinked away the spots, she realized that someone, Eric, was watching from the main house. Probably to confess to Blair, even though it was her fault. She'd been the one who'd leaned forward and put her lips on his. For all her confusion about tonight, that was one detail she was absolutely sure of.

Was he watching her from Blair's room? She was too flustered to count windows and figure out which room, but then it didn't matter anyway, did it? Blair would know by morning anyway.

Allan lifted her chin up to the starlight. "Are you okay? You look like a half-drowned kitten."

"Cats have nine lives, right? Hopefully, I have a few left."

She stumbled back to the most stable home she had ever had, stripped off her swimsuit and fell into bed despite her wet hair. Within a few minutes she was asleep but her dreams were of runaway roller coasters and tracks that ended but carts that kept going, flying through the air, free falling, falling, falling....

Until her alarm rang and she hit bottom.

Blair needs to see you when you're dressed. The text on her phone said it all.

She walked around her little apartment saying goodbye to the décor designed by one of San Francisco's up-and-comings just for her. Standing inside the closet that was bigger than her New Mexico bedroom, she ran her hands over the expensive material of her wardrobe. Her bathroom, big and bright with sunlight streaming through the skylights, had always been her favorite room. She debated on taking one last long soak in her deep whirlpool tub or one last pulsating shower under the four sunflower-large shower heads.

Was losing all this worth one kiss?

The bath would take longer and give her a few more minutes to surround herself in luxury, but she had too much nervous energy to relax and enjoy it.

Her chest was so tight she could hardly take a breath. Her shoulders ached, her head throbbed.

She was not in the best place to make a dignified exit. And she was determined to exit with dignity.

Selena had always prided herself on never popping a pill to relax. She had a different method that had always worked for her. If it would only work now, she could keep from being a mass of quivering nerves as Blair kicked her out the door.

She lit candles of lemon and lavender and turned off the overhead lights to enjoy the ambiance. The morning sun through the window dappled her vanity and cast animated shadows on the white marble of her walk-in shower.

As she worked the shampoo through her hair, she relived last night—every second of her fairy tale evening—right up to goodbye. She didn't want to think about her foolishness that had cost her the best job she'd ever had, not while she enjoyed her last morning in luxury.

The water became pulsating points of stimulation as they drenched her sensitive skin. Steam seeped into every pore and she inhaled, feeling herself open up. The soap made her skin slick and smooth. She adjusted a shower head and cranked up the pressure. She was so close, so close to release. Today, of all days, she needed the tension relief.

She closed her eyes and remembered how drowning in Eric's kiss had felt. She remembered the touch of his chest against hers. His heartbeat had been hard and strong and fast. With a little imagination she could think of him there with her. His hands would touch her along her face then down her throat. He would cup her breasts and rub his thumbs across her wet, swollen nipples. Then his hands would travel down her stomach to her curls. With a simple flick of his finger he would—

Yes! Her whole body shook. Feeling replaced thought. Feeling replaced water and air and time and place. She panted for breath and squeezed her thighs tighter as the pulsing grew and grew until she could no longer breathe.

Tension burst within her, sending shocks throughout her body. *Eric!*

Her legs shook so hard that she had to sit down on the shower floor. The two steps she needed to make to get to the built-in marble bench was beyond her abilities.

As her ragged breathing smoothed, she vaguely wondered if she had called Eric's name out loud or only in her head. Not that it mattered.

How much would she reveal to Blair when questioned? She would take the blame for whatever Eric had decided to confess but she wouldn't volunteer anything.

Maybe she was making too much of this. Eric flirted with a lot of women. According to the tabloids, he did a lot more than flirt.

But Blair was special. What Eric and Blair had between them was special. Everyone knew that. They had their own special arrangement—but that arrangement didn't include Blair's assistant. What if Eric said nothing to Blair about the kiss? But, then, why would he drive back in the middle of the night if not to confess?

And Selena couldn't act as if nothing happened. She couldn't look Blair in the eye, accept her money, accept her friendship and say nothing about that stolen kiss.

Unless it meant nothing to anyone but her.

She was so confused.

The water turned cold as it beat down upon Selena's head and shoulders. Her hair clung to her like slimy seaweed with gobs of conditioner gluing it to her back. Her foot, trapped under her thigh, started to throb and tingle.

Funny how throbbing and tingling had been the pleasurable sensations just a few moments ago. Now they meant pain.

Quickly, she scrubbed the conditioner from her hair then reached for her towel. She might be able to rub away her goose bumps along her arms and legs, but no amount of rubbing could warm the chill from her heart.

Knowing she was stalling, Selena took a few extra minutes with the blow dryer, coaxing her smooth, straight hair to flip under at the ends. From her closet, she choose her favorite jeans and a gauzy shirt that she hadn't worn yet and wrapped a thick leather belt around her waist, all the while thinking that these might be the only clothes she would be taking with her. She reached for her favorite two and one-half inch wedges but stopped herself. Today might call for a lot of pounding the pavement. Ballerina flats could take the stress better.

Since her wardrobe had been gifts from Blair, Selena would gladly leave it behind in atonement. If Eric had been *her* boyfriend, there would have been no polite text or waiting until morning. But then, Blair had more class than Selena ever would.

She applied her makeup like war paint, bright and bold with an extra coat of mascara, then went in search of Blair.

Instead she found Eric. He was in the kitchen, scrambling eggs. His smile was broad as he turned around toward her. Then he took a good look at her and sobered. He turned back to the stove to push the eggs with the spatula. "I saw you swimming last night. You were really working off some excess energy."

She put the kitchen table between them. "Have you talked to Blair?"

"Yeah, sure. Why are you whispering?" He poured a glass of orange juice and set it on the table near her, almost brushing her hand.

"Did you tell her about last night?"

"I told her—"

From the breakfast room, Blair called out, "Selena? Is that you?"

Too late to corroborate stories, now.

Selena marched into the breakfast room with her head held high.

Blair, Dominic and Allan were all huddled around the table. Both Dominic and Allan stared at her as she walked in.

Blair's back was to Selena but her swollen hands were flying as she talked. Dom sat silent and slightly pushed away from the table, while Allan dodged Blair's waving hands as he scrutinized a photo in the local gossip rag.

Allan looked from Selena to Blair the back to Selena again. "We might be able to make it work."

Blair turned in her chair and held up a few pages of newsprint. She greeted Selena with a genuine smile. "I hear someone had a good time last night."

That sounded friendly enough. Maybe Blair was giving her a chance to explain, or to confess. Selena didn't have an explanation.

Dominic stood and pulled out Selena's chair. She would miss his Southern manners. "Good morning."

Trying to read anything from Dominic's expression or voice was like trying to read from the Rosetta stone.

Selena slid into the chair and attempted to catch a solid glimpse of the grainy black-and-white photos in Blair's paper.

Eric came in, juggling two plates of eggs and her juice. He set a plate of eggs in front of her and another in the empty place next to her. From his pocket he pulled out two aspirin and put them next to her plate. "You might need these."

Did he think she had a hangover? Did he think she was drunk last night? Could she have been? Had she made more of last night than it really was? Eric *had* pushed her away in the end. And she did have a hell of a headache starting.

She took the aspirin.

Blair leaned close and asked, "How are you feeling this morning?"

What was going on here? They all seemed to be hanging on her answer. "I'm fine. And you?"

"Not as miserable as yesterday. But then, I've come up with a great distraction." Blair sent a quick glance at Eric, then Dom, before coming back to Selena. Then she laid the paper flat so that Selena could see last night's kiss in newsprint. Another shot showed her in the swimsuit, Allan in shadows at her feet, but next to it the photo of her and Eric in his car, implying that the man in the shadows was Eric.

Blair bit her bottom lip. "You don't have to do this if you don't want to."

Selena tried to make the mental leap but failed. "Do what?"

Blair became deadly serious, her eyes sharp and direct. "Eric is okay with it. He said it would be fun. But if you don't want to, then that's okay. We'll come up with another way."

"Uh, you'll have to give me a hint or two." Selena had been fired before, but this didn't sound like any of those conversations.

Afraid to ask, she did it anyway. "Do what?"

"Hang out with Eric and let the paparazzi take photos of you as if you were me."

"Do what?!?" Selena's imagination went into overload. She could grasp the meaning of hang out with Eric. The photo taking took place all the time. But the *as if you were me* part confused the hell out of her.

Dom pushed the orange juice in front of her. "No vodka in there, but I can find some if you want me to."

She sipped the juice to give herself a break to unscramble her thoughts. After downing half the glass, she realized she would need more time to sort this out. "Could you explain it to me again? And this time, go really slow. And use little words."

"You couldn't do anything up close like a red carpet movie premier but you could—" Blair absently scratched at her neck. Dominic pushed her hand away and she sent him a sideways glance full of irritation. "Help me think here."

Allan flipped through the rumor rag and pointed to a fuzzy photo of a starlet and her boy toy on a blanket on a beach. Without the caption, the two lovers would have been hard to name. "Something like this?"

"Yes, exactly!" Blair's eyes sparkled and she practically started bouncing in her chair. "We've already got reservations for the next few days in Palm Springs. You know the place, Eric. The Majestic. We've stayed there before."

He shrugged his shoulders. "I wouldn't mind going back."

Blair bounced so hard she sloshed her juice out of the glass. "This could really work. We've got one of the big suites with an outside veranda, right, Selina? Make sure it's on the thirty-first floor or higher, though, so the zoom lenses can't pick you up too well. Then you could...hmmm. What would I do?"

Dom leaned forward. "Watch reality shows until your eyeballs fried?"

"Okay, don't do whatever I would do." She stole Dom's toast and pointed it at Selena. "I know. You could dine on the balcony wearing something sexy.

Eric could feed you strawberries dipped in chocolate and you could—"

Eric held up his hand for Blair to stop. "Selena, love, we won't do anything you don't want to do. I promise." He turned his raised hand into a sign for a solemn pledge.

"Wait!" When had Selena left the real world behind and gotten lost in the house of illusions? If she didn't know better, she would swear the room was tilting and she was looking into a really strange, cloudy funhouse mirror. Except this wasn't very fun.

"Let me get this straight." She looked at Blair, "Did you just gave me carte blanche with your boyfriend?"

"Boyfriend? Eric?" Blair blinked like she was staring in that same distorted mirror and she couldn't get a clear focus, either. "Eric's not my boyfriend. That's just a media thing. All this time, how could you not have known?"

Selena leaned forward and opened her mouth to speak, shook her head when nothing came out, then tried again. "Okay. I'm going to be blunt here. Even before I came on the scene, you and Eric were an item. You went everywhere together. You still do. He flies in to see you when you're on tour. You have a room set up for him in your house. You're a couple."

Blair and Eric sat speechless, looking at each other then back to Selena. Allan decided he needed more juice.

As Selena became certain that this was not her kind of carnival, Dominic spoke. "Have you ever seen them kiss? Not a polite social kiss but an intimate one? Or do anything else that lovers would normally do?"

Blair's face started to splotch worse than ever. She reached over and pinched Dom on the arm. "Of course she hasn't, you dolt."

Selena searched her memories and couldn't find a single one that revealed Blair and Eric to be more than good friends. "Then what's the deal between you two?"

Eric toyed with his glass. "It's like this. When Blair started breaking into the big leagues, she started getting invitations for dates from different guys, some of them rather influential. She didn't always want to accept but was afraid of getting blackballed, so we decided that I would become her permanent escort and we let it out that she was no longer available."

"And when my faithful bodyguard reviewed our plan, he agreed that it was for the best to have *someone* out there in the public eye. Since he refused to do it, Eric graciously agreed." Blair grinned at Dominic.

Dominic scowled back.

Blair ignored him and turned her attention back to Eric and Selena. "Until I get a better offer, Eric has been courteous enough to be my arm-ornament. And he looks so good in a tux."

Selena knew she was still missing something, but at least the room wasn't spinning any faster. The important point was that Eric was free and clear. But what did that mean to her? Everything was happening too quickly to think.

Eric looked sheepish. "I like the parties."

Blair pointed her finger at him. "Admit it. The arrangement has come in handy for you, too, hasn't it, Eric?" She took a healthy bite of her eggs. "Once he got those mentions in Forbes and Vogue, he had the same problem with women crawling all over him."

He shrugged, neither confirming nor denying. Selena always admired a man who didn't kiss and tell.

Allan must have felt it was safe to rejoin the conversation. He took a long look at Selena then said, "I think we could pull it off, at least for a week or so."

Selena tried to interject some sanity into the conversation. "There's no way I could stand in for you, Blair. We're the same size, but we don't look anything alike."

Allan reached down under his seat and brought up a news clippings. He laid a grainy newsprint photo on the table. "That's not what this photographer thought."

Selena examined the photo of her and Eric in the car yesterday coming in from San Francisco, her baseball cap obscuring her hair and features. Next to it was the kiss. Her big sunhat hid most of her face but did nothing to shadow her lips pressed into Eric's. In both, she had been mistaken for Blair.

Selena still had some sanity, as the logical part of her brain pointed out that this was great publicity for the clothing line, but Blair's insanity was creeping in. In another part of her brain, a little voice was asking what it would be like to have all Blair's amenities and Eric, too.

Blair rustled her paper to get attention. "And remember the week before last. You used my 'vette to drop off the dry cleaning."

Selena thought back to that picture. She'd been driving Blair's vintage corvette, with the top down, of course. She'd been wearing shades and her hair had been stuffed under a hat to keep it from tangling in the wind.

Protectively, she reached for her hair.

Allan nodded as if he could read her thoughts. "It would have to go."

"It will always grow back. And you might enjoy being a bottle- blond for a few weeks." Blair clasped her chubby fingers together like she was praying. "Please, Selena, please. These hives could be the end of my career."

"I don't think a few weeks out of the spotlight would put you on the skids."

Blair named off a dozen shooting stars who had burned out in the last two or three years because they couldn't keep up the pace. "And now that new kid is making her way up the charts. The critics are already comparing her to me and I'm not always coming out on top."

Selena thought about the newest cut that had been released last week. "She *is* good."

She grabbed a hank of her dark brown hair and studied it as if she'd never seen it before. From somewhere deep inside, excitement started to grow. "I don't want to outright lie, but I don't mind letting the gossip rags draw their own conclusions."

Eric reached out to touch her hair, then pulled his hand away. "Selena, you don't have to do this."

"I'd only be half of this farce, Eric. What do you think about it?"

"To tell the truth, it sounds like fun to me. I wouldn't mind giving it a try."

This was getting too weird. She should say no. She should get up, walk away and never look back.

This fabulous lifestyle, the clothes, the parties, the people, would all be a blip in time—as she walked her homeless self up and down the streets of San Francisco.

With any luck, she could get her old job back. Wearing the red yarn wig and a blue striped bloomers wasn't that bad, was it? And the fast food managers would let her eat all the chicken samples she could gobble. Besides, chicken was very healthy.

She might regret this later, but, "I'm in, too."

Blair raised her glass for a toast. "Hurrah to a great adventure!"

Allan raised his glass readily enough as did Eric. Blair elbowed Dominic until he joined in. Selena raised hers high and clinked away, wishing she'd taken Dominic up on the offer of the vodka.

"Adventure!" Selena echoed, then slammed back the juice in one big gulp.

CHAPTER SEVEN

Another hunk of brown hair fell to the floor, fanning out across Blair's fake polar bear rug in her dressing room as Allan manned the scissors.

What have I done?

As if Blair could read her mind, she called through the louvered bathroom doors, "Thank you so much for this, Selena. You're saving my life."

Selena needed to remember that. She had Blair's gratitude. She had her job. And she had Eric. Well, sort of.

Until last night, she would have sworn that she and Eric were only acquaintances on the road to becoming good friends. But then, there was that kiss.

And what about her vow? What about her promise to be true to herself, especially in relationships? It was a hell of a lot easier to keep that vow when she could use Blair as an excuse. Now that the only thing holding her back was herself, she didn't know what she would do.

Too much, too fast. She'd experienced more ups and downs in the last few hours than she had felt on the tallest, fastest coaster she'd ever ridden.

Another snip. The floor was deep in snake-like locks.

Sitting with her back to the mirror, she could only judge Allan's progress by watching the results pile up at her feet.

Selena blinked back her tears before they spilled over.

Allan saw anyway. "It will be okay."

She wiped away a wet track down her cheek. "Um-hum." Words wouldn't work past the knot in her throat right now.

Selena gave herself a mental shake and focused on the positive. I get to keep my job. I'm getting paid mega-bucks. I'll be living the lifestyle of the rich and famous.

And Eric is unattached and up for grabs. Was that a positive or not?

"Allan, what do you know about Eric?"

He thought for a while, like he was sorting through bits and pieces, deciding which ones to give her. "He's nice." Allan snipped another lock. "He's rich."

"Yes, to both of those." If she just wanted nice and rich, she could have said yes to Wilhelm. She wanted more.

Allan sectioned off another section. "He's a good friend to Blair."

Selena was still having a hard time wrapping her mind around him not being part of a couple with Blair. For a year and a half she'd been part of Blair's retinue and close to Blair. Personal assistant couldn't get much closer. How could she not have known? Was it because she hadn't really wanted to know? Had her psyche been protecting her from another bad relationship?

"You're sure that's all he is? A platonic friend?" She had been completely convinced that Eric was part of Blair's retinue, too, playing the part of love interest.

Had it really all been in play? Just pretend and nothing more?

"Absolutely." Allan tilted her head down. "Be still a minute."

It was true that for weeks at a time, Eric might not show up, but the minute Blair had a big PR event, there he was.

While that fit with their story, he had also been around a lot when nothing was going on. Like the time he'd flown into Chicago when they'd had that three-day break in their schedule. Blair had slept a lot. Eric had hung with Selena, watching TV, doing Sudoku puzzles and waiting for Blair to wake up from her nap. If that wasn't devotion, she didn't know what was.

With her head bent down, she struggled to ask, "How long have they known each other?"

"Since before Blair started singing professionally. I'm not sure how long that's been." Allan held her ear down and snipped around it. The falling hair tickled.

"He certainly visits a lot. The minute we arrive home from tour, there he is on the doorstep."

"Yeah, it seems that way, doesn't it. He's only been doing that recently, though, after Blair hit the charts. Before that we'd only see him a couple of times a month when they did the party scene together." Allan tilted Selena's head the other direction and began snipping around her other ear.

"Honestly, I don't know when he gets his own work done. But from the way everyone spoke of him at his party, he must be very good at it."

Allan answered with a distracted mumble.

Maybe Eric didn't sleep. There were some people who didn't. She always wondered if they even bothered going to bed to keep up appearances.

Apparently, Eric only appeared to sleep with Blair and really didn't.

What would Eric be like in bed? His mouth was hot. So were his hands. What about the rest of him? And there it led, back to sex. Sex always got her in the wrong place with the wrong person.

Selena had been completely wrong too many times.

"Selena, you've got to sit still. I don't want to jab you in the neck with these scissors."

"Oh, sorry." And maybe about this scheme she had just agreed to. This whole charade thing should feel wrong. But it didn't. It felt like that moment when she sat at the top of the tallest peak of Big Sur waiting for the climax and knowing that the big plunge would take her breath away.

Yup, her judgment was completely shot.

Allan yanked a strand of hair and Selena winced.

"Sorry. You might feel a tug while I razor the ends."

"It's okay. I'm tough."

"Yeah, you are. And don't you ever forget it."

He tilted her head down and tugged along her nape.

Sticking to her vow was the safe plan. Her next relationship would be a real one. There was no way she could find love for herself when she played another woman.

Cool air chilled her bare neck. That's when she realized how short her hair would be. What would she look like when this was done? A parody of Blair? A warped and ugly copy?

She let out a sigh, blowing hair off her nose.

"You okay?" Allan lifted her head and pulled little sprigs around her forehead.

"I'm all right." And she *would* be all right. Selena always landed on her feet. Like now. She had her job, had her pride, and, after this farce was over, she would have a nice enough bank account to cushion her when this wild ride was over.

This topsy-turvy scheme needed to work. If it didn't, the end of the ride might come sooner than anyone anticipated for all of them.

Blair wasn't experiencing the paranoia so many artists fell prey to when she worried about how her hives could affect her career. Her fears were valid. The one solid lesson Selena had learned in her last eighteen months was that staying on top was more about buzz than talent.

Not only could Blair's singing career wither away, but her clothing line would flop and she had invested a good chunk of change there.

"Almost done in there?" Eric called through the door.

She could hear him pace as Blair fussed at him to settle down and help her come up with some long distance photo ops.

Was he having second thoughts?

Allan stopped tugging. "No. It will be a while. Go away."

"I could do this on my own, without Eric."

"I don't know how successful you'd be. Obscure photos of single celebs don't garner half the attention that couples do." Allan tugged and pulled around her hairline. "Besides, they're only confusing you for her when you're out with Eric."

"Maybe. But then, they're used to seeing Blair with you and Dom and Eric."

"My point. Couple pictures, even with bodyguards, play better than single pics. Unless the star is doing something stupid, or course."

Allan hummed under his breath. It took a few bars for Selena to recognize the song as the new one that had just knocked Blair off the charts. It was a hard, driving tune, easy to dance to. It was one of those songs where everything came together.

Blair hadn't had a hit like that since Roses and her upcoming releases didn't hold any promises. They weren't bad. They just didn't have that extra spark that made a song rise to the top position on the charts.

Thinking back, Selena realized Blair had been exhausted the whole time she had been recording and her lack of energy showed.

Publicity was the key, at least until the clothing line launched.

Being out of the spotlight, especially for a stress-induced illness, could start a fast downward spiral. Selena would make this work. She had to, not only for her job for Blair's whole enterprise.

The responsibility scared the shit out of her. At least, Eric would be there. Knowing Eric would be a part of this should have settled her nerves. Instead, her stomach started to flutter.

Allan ruffled through her hair, "Shake your head, darling."

His fake Vidal Sassoon accent was awful but his tone was cheerful and confident.

"Now for the color." He blew into a pair of surgical gloves to stretch them, then worked them onto his large hands with practiced ease.

The bleach smelled sharp. Sharp enough to melt the hair off her head, at least the hair she had left.

She closed her eyes and pictured herself as Marilyn Monroe in Gentlemen Prefer Blondes. Yes, she could see herself playing Marilyn's role of Lorelei Lee. If she could think of this whole thing as a comedy, she could pull it off.

"Who taught you to color hair, Allan?"

"Why? Worried?"

"Hell, yeah. It's not every day that my boss's bodyguard gives me a makeover."

He brushed a big, wet glop onto her head. The glop was cold and pungent as he spread it across her scalp. "My mom is a hairdresser in L.A."

Selena shivered as her head chilled. "Pretty high fashion stuff in L.A., right? I guess you gained a lot of experience with cut and color there."

"I used to sweep the shop during the summers when I was in junior high."

"You mean I'm your first?"

"Are you calling me a virgin?"

"Well? Are you?"

"Live and learn. That's my motto." With a flourish, he shook open a plastic cap and popped it onto her head. "Now for the wait."

He set an egg timer, handed her a magazine she'd already read, *Like in a real salon*, he said, and left.

To pass the time, Selena filed her nails to keep from biting them, shaping her long, expensive nail tips down to barely-there crescents.

She held them up to inspect them. Blair kept her nails short and bare for playing guitar. Now Selena's were just like Blair's. Not that anyone should get close enough to see her nails. If anyone did discover the switch, how would she and Blair explain their body- double act?

As soon as the egg timer beeped, Selena hit the shower. This new hair would take some getting used to. She used too much shampoo and her fingers scrubbed though air more than hair. A quick buff with the towel was all it took to keep water from dripping into her eyes and down her back. The whole process was quicker than expected. She decided to call it a plus.

Now for the moment of truth. She turned to face the mirror.

Oh, wow! Were those her cheekbones? Her darker eyebrows really framed her face, making her eyes stand out. Did they really turn up at the corners and sparkle like that?

The short strands of white-blond hair tried to bend into gentle curls giving her a freshly tumbled look. She liked the softness. Not Blair-like, though. Blair's hair gel took care of the curl. Selena scrunched and straightened until spikes stuck up everywhere. The ragged texture played against her skin so it looked fresh and clear. Her natural complexion appeared tan against her pale hair.

She couldn't resist putting her own touch on the style, though, and pulled some wisps forward so that they framed her face. If the cameras got close enough to notice the difference, the game would be up anyway.

What would happen if this fell through? Selena could think of all kinds of dire consequences.

She would just have to make it work. Failure was not an option.

Of course, new hair color meant new makeup. Blair certainly had enough to share. The two bottom drawers of her vanity were filled with unopened cosmetics, often sent by some ambitious company hoping Blair would endorse them.

Selena laid out a couple of blushes, lip colors and eye shadows to try.

Pink. She'd never gone with pink before. She chose a palette with coral undertones and a lipstick called Walk on the Wild Side. The high gloss color gave her a luscious pout that looked as if she'd just been kissed.

Would Eric try to kiss her again? Would she let him? Would he see the real Selena under her disguise or would he be kissing the Blair stand-in? She still had a hard time thinking he didn't have feelings for Blair. A man didn't hang around as much as he did if he wasn't in lust if not in love.

Could it be unrequited love on his part? But what about last night? Is that what happened last night? She had been a substitute for Blair? Were they both caught up in the moment?

A persistent, niggling voice in her conscience told her that she was selling Eric short. While he might enjoy a passionate moment as well as the next man, he had more respect for her than to use her as a substitute for Blair. But was it only a customary, goodnight kiss after a pleasant evening together? It had felt like more.

Or did she just want it to be more?

Only yesterday, when she had thought Eric was unavailable, they had been friends, barely past the acquaintance stage. Now, with this imposed closeness, they had the opportunity to become good friends or, at least, good lovers.

Deep inside, she had a hunch Eric would be an awesome lover. Squash that! Her last hunch had ended up with her homeless. She would never sleep on the couch again.

No. She deserved something special, something meant just for her. She would not fall back into old habits of being grateful for whoever would take her. She would not be her mother.

The cycle would end with her.

In the meantime, she had agreed to this job and she would get on with it. And she would enjoy the hell out of it, too. This would be just like the rollercoaster at Big Sur. Fast, scary and, if she didn't pay attention, over before she knew it. *Hands in the air, Selena. Here comes the first big drop.*

She choose a fuchsia and orange sundress from Blair's closet. The colors went with her makeup and made the best of her warm skin tone. In a retro fifties style, the dress had a V-neck and a scooped back.

Eric had seemed to appreciate her bare back last night. Not that it mattered. The time for fantasies had ended at midnight.

That didn't mean she couldn't dress for success, though. Fun and glamorous was the focus of Blair's line and Selena would do her best to promote it, if only from a distance.

She gathered her assets and adjusted them in the built-in bra, plumping and gathering until her cleavage looked as deep as the Grand Canyon. The fuchsia wedges that had been dyed to match had her standing on her tiptoes, giving her a lean, leggy silhouette in the full length mirror.

She stared at herself, trying to reconcile the new sexy celeb look-a-like that stared back with the Selena that she had always been. They said that blondes had more fun. She would do her best to prove them right.

Let the party begin!

When she finally emerged, no one waited for her. *What did you expect, Selena? Throngs in the hallways with wolf whistles and cat calls?* She had to admit that she had at least hoped for one interested party. She would not think about which particular one she had hoped for.

She found Dominic and Blair in the office. Dominic sat hunched over the computer and Blair lay on the couch leafing through gossip rags. A new layer of welts coated half her face and neck and her eyes were swollen.

She framed herself in the doorway and cleared her throat. "Well? What do you think?"

Blair sat up, wincing with the effort. "Oh, Selena, you look so—so different."

"Different good or different bad?"

"Wonderful. You look wonderful. Not that you haven't always looked very nice." Blair bit her knuckle. She got up from the couch and walked toward Dominic as if for support. "I'm not doing this well. Selena, you are a beautiful woman and you look fantastic. You have such flair about you. And I am so grateful. You're saving my life."

Dominic frowned as he studied the hair, the dress, the legs, and finally the shoes. "From a distance, you'll do."

It was all Selena could do to keep from bursting into tears, or throwing something, or both. She covered with sarcasm. "Gee, thanks."

Blair elbowed him and he reconsidered his response. "You look very nice."

His *very nice* wasn't nearly as enthusiastic as Blair's *fantastic*. Grudgingly, Selena gave him Brownie points for going against his nature and trying to be polite.

Blair looked down at her oversized sleep shirt and gym shorts. "I'm going to have a hard time living up to my own image now. I'm just thankful I'll have an image to promote. You are such a good friend, Selena. I'll owe you forever."

Dominic said, "We've got to make it successful first."

Mister Sunshine at his finest. Did the man ever say anything positive? Why did Blair keep him around? Bodyguards were a dime a dozen.

Who needed male appreciation anyway?

"Uh, where's Eric?" Her voice was a little squeakier and a little sharper than usual, but then, she'd had a trying morning. Of course, she wanted to know strictly from a practical viewpoint. He was her partner in crime. If he didn't think her disguise was good enough to pull this off, she needed to know now.

Blair waved her pudgy hand. "He's off somewhere with Allan. They're coming up with photo ops for the two of you. He says he'll be ready in a few hours." She turned to the computer screen and started reading. "Beautiful sunsets, huh?"

Dom bent over to look at the screen with her. "Only a few hours away."

"Already?" Sidetracked by the makeover, Selena hadn't given much thought about timeline or logistics. "I guess I need to make arrangements to get us to Palm Springs. If we take his Gallardo and keep the top up—"

Blair swiveled around from the keyboard. "Eric's already taken care of that. He made arrangements to fly the two of you to Palm Springs. He called earlier about getting his plane fueled and filing a flight plan and whatever else pilots do before a flight."

"His plane?"

Dominic frowned. "Driving would take most of the night. You're not afraid of flying, Selena. You've flown all over the country with Blair."

"I'm not crazy about little planes."

"Don't worry, honey. Eric's plane isn't that small. What kind is it, Dom?"

"It's a Citation X, a jet. I've flown with Eric before. From what I can tell, he's a competent pilot." He reached over Blair's shoulder and tapped a key. Under his breath he added, "And he's got the best toys I've ever seen."

Selena hadn't felt this disoriented since she rode the Tilt-A-Whirl drunk. She sat on the couch and tried not to upchuck. "You made all this happen while I got a haircut and color?"

"I thought of most of it. Eric and Dominic helped, of course." Blair looked way too pleased with herself, as if she'd just figured out the secret passages in the House of Mirrors and now planned to lead unsuspecting dupes inside and leave them there.

Dominic shut down the computer and glanced at his watch. "You haven't slept at all this morning. Pills and bed in thirty minutes."

Blair patted his hand. "Nag."

The man had his softer side, at least where Blair was concerned.

He handed Selena a slip of paper with a phone extension she didn't recognize. "I've chartered a midnight flight with a discreet friend of mine. Blair needs to be well rested."

"Blair, you're going somewhere? You're supposed to be in bed."

"I can't stay here if I'm supposed to be in Palm Springs. What if one of our photographer friends spotted me? Dom has convinced me that I'll get better faster if I take a vacation. So, Cabo San Lucas, here we come."

Allan came into the office, a big grin on his face. "Everything's all set. One of our guys will come by a couple of times a day to make sure the house stays secure."

Selena's world was spinning out of control. She checked her watch. It wasn't even eleven yet and she was exhausted.

Allan gave Blair a big hug. "You take it easy and get well."

"And you take care of that pregnant lady of yours." Blair gave him a mock stern frown. "Whatever she wants, you just say, 'Yes, ma'am,' and everything will work out all right.

"Yes, ma'am." He tweaked a wild lock of Blair's hair. But then, Blair's hair was always wild. And now, so was Selena's. Selena reached up to confirm her spikes were still up there.

"Uh-uh. Don't touch." Then Allan took a long look at her. "Mmmm-mmmm, you are looking fine. I would take all the credit, but I had a lot to work with."

"Thanks." She gave him a hug. "Have fun."

"You, too. I'll see all of you in a couple of weeks."

Allan's footsteps plopped down the hallway, then stopped.

"Where's the party?" Eric ask. Hearing his voice made her knees weak. What would he think?

"The office," Allan answered. "Check out Selena's hair. It's killer."

"I liked it the way it was."

Great. Doesn't that just give me a warm fuzzy?

Blair tugged Dominic's hand. "Come on. Nap time."

They crowded the door so that Eric had to wait for them to clear the room before he could enter.

He stopped, several feet away from her and stared.

Selena stood in the middle of the room, arched an eyebrow and waited.

Eric moved closer, inspecting her like a bug. Would he stomp her or let her live?

She twirled for him, making sure he saw the low cut back of her dress. "Well?"

"You can carry off any look you try."

Okay, that compliment didn't gush but it didn't suck, either. "Let's just hope the media goes for my Blair look.

"I let the Majestic know we wanted to use the private entrance today. Blair reminded me that you always make the rooms in your name. She also said I should cancel yours and stay with you in the suite since the whole point of our act is to keep the buzz going." He didn't meet her eyes. "We won't go anywhere you don't want to go."

Damn, he was sweet.

Where she wanted to go had nothing to do with where she shouldn't go. But she appreciated his reminder that she was in control.

Feeling like she had finally grabbed the brake on this runaway rollercoaster, she nodded her agreement. "Good approach."

She thumbed her phone. "I've got so many appointments to reschedule. I hope I can be as efficient and discreet. Then I need to go through Blair's closet and pack for both of us."

"Sure, no problem. We've got a couple of hours before we need to leave."

A couple of hours? To be gone indefinitely? She thought about panicking until she realized her deadline was exactly what she needed to keep her mind off the uncertain days ahead of her. She would work with the adrenaline while it lasted.

For the next two hours, Selena picked out clothes for her and Blair to fit any occasion either of them might find themselves in. At first, she folded the delicate silks and sequins with tissue paper in between the layers. As the clock ticked, she ended up shoving denim and knit into duffel bags.

They set off for the airport and Eric's private hanger only thirty minutes behind schedule. Selena regretted not being able to put the top down on Eric's car in case an ambitious photographer focused in on a clear shot. The more sedate form of travel would be the first of many that emphasized she couldn't be herself anymore.

As they pulled into Eric's parking slot, Blair flipped down the sun visor once again to stare at her new look. It shouldn't matter if she'd dyed her hair purple and put a ring thought her nose—though, thank heaven that wasn't the look Blair currently sported—as long as she knew who she was on the inside.

But then, maybe she'd always deluded herself.

While Eric did his visual inspection of his plane, she buckled into the right seat. She'd never sat in the cockpit of a plane before. This promised to be quite a ride.

Eric climbed aboard and handed her a headset. "Put these on and you can listen to the tower."

When she couldn't get the set adjusted, he reached over and adjusted it for her and repositioned the mouthpiece. His thumb traced a line along her mouth. "You okay?"

"Yeah, sure." The mouthpiece bumped her lip.

He put on his own headset. "Can you hear me?"

"Yes." This would be fun. Really it would. She wished Eric would touch her again, but his hands were busy flipping switches and his eyes were busy checking the gauges.

He spoke to the tower in a language that barely resembled English, then maneuvered his plane to the head of the runway. "Off we go." His voice sounded in her ear.

"To adventure."

"Here, here." He revved the engine and they sped down the runway faster and faster, until the ground fell away beneath them.

Selena spent the next hour and a half staring out the window, making sure the wings didn't fall off the plane.

The sun was setting as they landed on the strip reserved for private planes. Eric taxied to a community hangar with a huge helicopter and a small prop plane inside.

"We're here, safe and sound." He reached over and took her headset off. "That wasn't too bad, was it?"

"You're a good pilot."

He winked. "That's not all I'm good at."

This was the kind of teasing she and Eric had always shared. But this time, she could act on it. "Yeah? What's your specialty?"

Before he could answer, a limousine pulled up to the hangar and a chauffeur in a black suit stepped out.

"Here we go." Eric reached behind the seat and handed Selena the oversized purse she'd packed for this occasion.

Selena pulled out the sheer scarf, wrapped it around her head and tied it under her chin. She fluffed it out so that it covered much of her jaw line. Dark glasses covered the top half of her face. "This feels silly."

"Very glamorous. Like a fifties movie star."

"Thanks."

Eric handed the bags down the three short steps to the driver who waited at the door, then he motioned for Selena to descend. With her dark glasses and scarf obscuring her vision, she stumbled on the bottom step.

"Ma'am." The driver held out his hand to help her in.

Great. Now Blair would get the reputation as a lush. She muttered, "Thanks," before she realized he might know Blair's voice. *Whoa, there Selena. You're getting a little too caught up in this aren't you?* What were the odds the driver would recognized Blair's speaking voice when most people had only heard her sing?

The drive to the hotel was short, eventless and silent so the driver wouldn't notice Selena's lack of a California accent. They made it through the back entrance and into the elevator without mishap. Selena started to take off her scarf when Eric put his hand on her arm. He pointed up to a tiny camera lens in the roof of the elevator car.

"Security."

Selena sighed. She was already earning every penny of her bonus.

CHAPTER EIGHT

The suite was extravagant, but it had been intended to serve double duty as a backdrop for Blair's interview with Entertainment Tonight and a prop room for the photo shoot for Seventeen magazine.

Selena had done some fancy talking to get those appointments postponed. She'd finally just told the truth. Blair's doctor had ordered rest and relaxation. She had hinted that Blair had strained her voice, a condition that everyone in Celebrityville understood. Because Blair had never canceled before, she would hopefully escape any ill-will this time.

After the scarf, sunglasses and stumbling bit, the driver was probably spreading the word about anything from plastic surgery to rehab. Another condition everyone in Celebrityville understood.

Selena whipped off her concealing accessories. "Such a modest little home-away-from-home."

"What's that?" Eric squeezed in behind her with their carry-ons.

"This is a lot more excessive than the suites we usually get. I sure as hell hope our ploy works and Blair makes lots of money on her upcoming clothing line. She'll need it if she gets used to this." Selena rubbed her forehead. "If I get used to this. Damn. This is getting confusing already."

Eric left her at the door to put their bags in the bedroom. She noted that he deposited *both* their bags in the room with a solitary bed.

The bed, a huge custom-sized four poster, sat on a dais in the middle of the bedroom. In the whole spacious suite, it was the only piece of furniture that could be comfortably slept on.

What was he expecting?

Eric came back, found her standing in the exact same place, then moved behind her and rested a comforting arm on her shoulder. "What do you think?"

What did she think? She was too busy feeling to think. All it would take was a one hundred and eighty degree turn. She would be face-to-face, mouth-to-mouth, pelvis-to-pelvis with one of the best men she had ever met.

You're in control, he had promised her, and she believed him. Nothing would happen without her wanting it. But exactly what did she want?

Eric tried again. "This is quite a room, isn't it?"

Selena swallowed and attempted to discipline her thoughts. "Yes. It is."

The furniture of the suite was museum quality. The straight-backed wing chairs made relaxed posture impossible and the ornately carved loveseat, with its tufted covering, didn't look like it was made for sitting on, much less sleeping.

She had meant it when she had sworn off couches forever.

Eric wasn't going to like sleeping on the couch much. Yup, that little antique settee was going to really test the bonds of Eric's and Blair's friendship.

And, yes, she could invite him to share the bed.

But she had sworn to herself that her next relationship would be a solid, true melding of the spirits as well as the bodies. And if she had to walk away from it, she could walk away with dignity. Not with her clothes spilling onto the concrete through a tear in an old grocery sack.

All this swearing she had been doing lately put Eric on the short end of the stick again.

She shuddered. Never again would she be homeless, especially because of a man.

Eric rubbed her arms. "Are you cold?

His concern warmed her, all the way to her heart and other cold places. "I'm fine."

"Yes. You are." He said it with a mock leer, the same kind of teasing he would have done before the kiss. If Selena hadn't known him so well, she wouldn't have noticed the strain in his voice.

Eric *was* a good man. He was the kind of man any woman would be wise to fall for. The kind of man any woman would be thanking her lucky stars to be cloistered in a magnificent hotel with. The kind of man to make her question her resolutions and her sanity for keeping them.

His fingers trickling down her bare arms made her feel so alive, so excited, so wanted.

She steeled herself to think with ice-crystal clear logic. What did this touching mean? What did *she* mean to Eric?

Her logic reminded her that she wanted to mean more than a weekend fling. Her body cried out differently.

With more will-power than she knew she had, she pulled away.

"I wonder if this loveseat is as uncomfortable as is looks." Deep inside, her intuition argued with her logic about Eric being different. But her logic reminded her intuition that it had been wrong before.

Eric followed her into the sitting area. "Stiff and extremely uncomfortable. Makes you wonder about what kind of love these things are named after."

If he expected an erect penis joke here, he was out of luck. The internal battle Selena was fighting left no room for their normal good-natured bantering.

He must have read something scary on her face because he quickly diverted to the French doors separating the room from the balcony, putting space between them.

He cleared his throat. "Does it smell stale in here to you? Do you mind if I open these?"

"Go ahead." She shifted on the rock-hard loveseat. It was even worse than it looked.

Eric would be a good lover. Considerate. Fun.

Her last boyfriend had been a stand-up comic. But he was only funny on stage. Off-stage, he was a hard drinking, brooding artist who tried to put her on the street. His new girlfriend had saved her.

Gina had felt embarrassed when she found out that Selena was not only still in the picture, she was still in the apartment, with no idea that her boyfriend was done with her.

Since Gina had been moving among friends for over a year, she knew the value of having a roof over her head and offered the couch as graciously as she could. Playing the comic, he had made a stupid, cutting joke about a threesome but Selena hadn't told him what to do with it. Instead, she had swallowed her pride and accepted Gina's compassion and charity.

Never again.

Eric called from the balcony, "The view is fantastic. Come look."

"Can't. Not until twilight. A long lens could snap a shot and the game would be over before we even got started good." Pushing her personal problems out of the way to concentrate on work felt good. Her brain kicked in and sent her libido back into solitary confinement.

Eric came back in. "Blair has no idea what a great friend she has in you."

Friends. That was the answer. Lovers could be found on any street corner. Eric had too much friend-potential, and friends were too hard to come by. In fact, Selena had never had a male friend.

With all the hours they would spend together, they had a chance to get to know each other well. That's what she would do. They would talk, share, laugh together and really get to know each other.

She would devote this whole incarceration to becoming friends with Eric. And whenever that horny little voice inside whispered about more than friends, she would remember the grocery sack with the hole in it.

She looked around their velvet prison and tried not to think of perfect seduction ploys.

Let the deep, meaningful conversations begin!

Selena's stomach growled. Lunch had been half a bag of Peanut M&Ms of undetermined expiration date that she'd found in her purse. She'd bet that Eric's half hadn't lasted any longer than hers.

The welcome basket overflowed with chocolates and fruit. She tossed Eric an apple and chose a golden-brown Asian pear that dripped juice as she bit into it.

"Thanks." He bit with one hand and opened the door to a huge built-in armoire with the other. There it was. The number one destroyer of communication between men and women. A big screen TV.

Within two seconds, Eric scooped up the remote from the gold-leaf and glass coffee table and flipped it on.

And then that damned box stole away all of his attention and all her chances of meaningful friendship talk. Eric pushed the coffee table away, grabbed up the bazillion-dollar-a-piece throw pillows, arranged them on the Oriental rug and plopped down on the floor.

"Might as well get used to it down there," she mumbled.

"What?"

She raised her voice over the sports announcer's annoying cheer. "Do you think we could dine on the balcony? It would be the perfect setup for the paparazzi and—"

A knock on the door interrupted her.

Eric looked through the peephole. "Bellboy."

"I think I'll take a bath while they unpack us."

"Okay. What do you want from room service?"

The knock sounded again.

"I don't know. Order for me, okay?"

On her way into the bathroom, she snagged the welcome basket. She thought about leaving an orange on the table for Eric, but then changed her mind. If he got hungry, he could eat the remote.

A collection of bottles lined the shelf above the baby grand-sized tub. The huge picture window that made up the back wall of the tub enclave overlooked the mountains. Selena adjusted the water and added a few drops of lavender-scented oil. Not dramatic enough.

She found a bottle of bubble bath, sniffed it and decided that the verbena wouldn't clash with the lavender and dumped in several large globs. The heady aroma floated on the steam, filling the room.

Tea light candles sat along the ledge of the tub, waiting to be lit. With the overhead lights dimmed, they flickered, casting shadows on the walls. The setting was out of a movie.

Of course, in the movies, the male lead usually walked in on the leading lady.

She peeled off the fuchsia dress that had served her so well and lowered herself into hot water up to her neck before turning off the faucet.

With a push of the button, the water around her began to churn. Bubble, bubble, boil and trouble. What have you gotten yourself into, Selena Maria?

The hot water eased the stress from her shoulders and her neck. She adjusted the bath pillow so thoughtfully provided, closed her eyes and relaxed for the first time since kissing Eric on the stairs of his estate last night.

At the memory of his kiss, her lips tingled and she rubbed them with her wet finger.

Was she being an idiot? Here she was in the perfect setting with only a louvered door separating her from a gorgeous man.

She felt so lonely. And so alone. And it had been so long. Was Eric as lonely too out there?

This friendship thing was just a foolish dream. Lasting relationships only happened in Hallmark movies and romance novels. How many women dreamed of opportunities like this one? How could she even think of letting it go for some stupid higher purpose that didn't even exist?

What would he do if she called for him? Would he come for her?

She took a big bite out of an apple and set it on the rim of the tub, setting the stage. Down through time, man had not been able to resist such a tempting offer.

"Eric?" Nothing.

Maybe a bit louder. "Eric?"

The sports announcer said something discernible in his cheerful ex-jock voice and the crowd cheered. So did Eric.

"No! Don't throw it away! Run! Run!" Eric yelled at the big screen. She heard a pillow hit the TV.

Don't throw it away. How prophetic.

The cheerful announcer shouted, "Look at that interception. What great hands! He's going all the way. Look at that! Touchdown. There will be rejoicing in Chicago tonight."

Amidst all the background noise, a less cheerful announcer droned, "You can blame it on the weak defense."

Weak defense. Yup. That's why Selena always lost the game. Well, she wouldn't lose this time.

Damn! Saved by the Bears.

Her strenuous use of willpower left her exhausted. Not that her late, restless night didn't factor in too. So much had happened in the last twenty-four hours.

She stretched and yawned. It would feel so good to close her eyes for a moment.

The game ended and hunger pains attacked Eric again. He couldn't believe Selena had taken the whole basket into the bathroom with her. With room service backed up, dinner wouldn't show up for another hour and a half.

He had tried to use his annoyance with her hoarding all the food to keep from thinking of her naked, with only a thin wall separating her from him. Then he had tried to use the game to distract him from offering to scrub her back.

But his hunger triggered an even more primitive need.

He forced the caveman back into his cave long enough to realize that beneath all the guttural stuff was a nagging worry.

How long had it been since he'd heard noise from the bathroom?

"Selena?" Eric knocked on the louvered doors. "Selena, are you okay?"

The only sound he could hear was the roar of the whirlpool. He should check on her. He pushed against the doors, held them open a few inches and listened.

"Selena?"

Nothing.

This could be bad. She could be drowning, or already under.

He shoved open the door, trying to keep his mind on Selena's well-being instead of on seeing her naked.

Naked won.

Selena lay in the tub with her head back on a bath pillow. The steam had turned her new haircut into a riot of curls. Her eyelids twitched delicately from dreams he could only fantasize about. Her beautiful long neck lay exposed, begging him to trail kisses along its length. Her mouth fell open as if inviting his own mouth to cover it.

An apple with a bite missing sat by her outflung hand, mocking him. Obviously, she had satisfied her hunger without him.

He took a step forward, ramming his foot into the door. The noise didn't even make her flinch in her sleep, which was a damned good thing. Now that he saw she obviously wasn't drowning, how could he explain that he'd been staring, mesmerized, unable to escape the spell she cast over him in her sleep?

The drowning excuse wouldn't hold water. *Sheesh, that was bad.* It was the sort of pun Selena would giggle about. It was the kind of thing they both enjoyed.

When they made love, he would make sure they both enjoyed that, too.

"When, Eric? Not if?" caveman Eric asked from the most primitive cortex of his brain.

It's tricky, he argued with his baser self. If I had met her at a party, or on a wine tour, or anywhere except in the employment of my best friend, this whole situation would be different. I can't put her in an awkward place if she's not interested in me. And, except for that kiss, she doesn't even seem to be aware that I'm alive.

Foam bubbled around her, playing peek-a-boo with her luscious body. He could only catch teasing, watery glimpses of full breasts with large, dark aureoles, and long, long legs. One foot broke the surface of the water, propped on a molded indentation in the tub. He'd never had a foot fetish before but he was more than willing to develop one. His fingers itched to trace her arch, then up around her ankle, then higher along her calf to the inside of her thigh, then....

All right, Mr. Voyeur, that's enough ogling an unaware woman. Your grandmother taught you better. His conscience could kick in at the most inopportune times.

Using all his willpower, he backed out of the bathroom and back to the TV.

Selena listened to the door click shut, then for Eric's footfalls in the lush carpet as he walked away. She stretched, feeling as sensuous as a cat. How long had he watched her? She wanted to call him back. But then what?

Why hadn't he awakened her?

Maybe he just wasn't that into her.

Maybe he hadn't liked what he had seen.

The water suddenly felt cold, making her shiver. She stepped out and watched the bubbles swirl down the drain.

Where she had been so excited about the luxury surrounding her, the thick towels now felt rough and scratchy as she dried herself. The expensive lotion lay sticky on her skin. The candles overpowered her with their heady scent as she blew them out.

She took a look at herself in the mirror, feeling the need to be beautiful. Her short hair startled her, making her eyes look bigger than usual.

Mascara and a nice thick eyeliner would make them look even bigger.

Ignore her, would he?

A wicked smile crept out. A little vamping never hurt anyone.

She applied her makeup with a heavy hand. Bright red on her lips, thick liner on her eyelids and a fake beauty mark right at the corner of her mouth gave her that movie star quality she was going for. She reached for the gel to straighten her curls, then decided against it. The curls looked softer, more touchable, more in keeping with the femme fatale she wanted to be tonight.

If this media ploy worked the way it should, Blair would end up with a more glamorous image whether she wanted it or not.

Selena heard a knock on the door and the rattle of a dinner cart moving out to the veranda. Delicious smells wafted past the closed bedroom door.

The white dress *a la* Marilyn Monroe and the silver strappy sandals would be perfect. Sparkly Austrian crystal earrings as big as chandeliers played up her newly discovered cheekbones and the matching necklace dipped right between her breasts, almost to her waist where the halter top ended and the waistband of the dress began. The dress was open backed, of course. She would use every advantage she could find. Yes, tonight she would find out if blondes really did have more fun.

She had learned her seduction skills from the best. Selena had never lost a man she intended to have and she wasn't about to start tonight.

Selena took one final look in the full length mirror—and detested the woman looking back at her.

What was she doing? She hadn't gone after a guy just to score points since high school. Back then, her goal had been to seduce the captain of every team, including the chess team, hoping to find whatever her mother kept looking for in a man.

She had learned since then, hard lessons, painful lessons, about finding what she needed in herself. And now she was playing some game, pretending to be someone she wasn't, so she could score a point.

This wasn't her. This wasn't someone she wanted Eric to meet.

She looked in the mirror again. New hair color, new clothes and new makeup didn't mean new Selena. She searched her eyes and searched her heart. What did she really want?

She wanted dignity, self-confidence and respect.

And she could have that with Eric. He wouldn't demand kisses for conversation or sex for friendship.

What else do you want? her conscience asked. She took a deep breath and plunged.

She wanted a relationship with Eric. Not one based on lust, but one built from true caring and maybe even love—whatever love was.

Love? Whoa, there, little miss. It's a mighty big step from the kiddie coasters to the dark and scary rides.

"Selena?" Eric called through the door. "Dinner's ready and the coast is clear."

"I'm coming." Tonight, she would start with dinner and splurge on dessert. Then she would see where this relationship thing went.

While the sitting room was dressed to impress, the balcony was decorated to enjoy. Through the open curtains of the sitting room's French doors, lights blinked from the city below. The doors opened easily. A perfect breeze blew across the balcony, warm and playful enough to make the curtains swing. A large dining table and matching chairs took up one corner of the balcony, while a collection of deeply cushioned teak reclining chairs, one of them wide enough for two, took up the other corner.

The setting was perfect for an *al fresco* tryst. She didn't have to use much imagination at all to picture her and Eric finishing what they had started last night on his stairs. Even without the privacy screening on either end of the balcony, they wouldn't be disturbed by neighbors, since Selena had rented the rooms to either side of them.

Eric stood as soon as she walked onto the balcony. "Wow. You are stunning."

She could really get used to his old world manners. He made her feel so treasured.

"Thanks." Her voice came out huskier than she had intended. She blamed her lack of control on stress. Too much had happened in the last few hours for her to keep a tight rein on her emotions. She walked past him to stare into the dusky sunset and find her poise.

She looked out at the pinks and oranges of the fading sun. "Nice, huh?"

Eric moved to stand beside her. "Yes. Beautiful."

He looked at her as he said it.

She strained to keep herself from moving forward, from brushing those lips she had tasted last night. Her fingernails dug into her palms.

She rolled her neck to break his stare. "Do you realize that this time last night you were making a toast to your grandmother? So much has happened between now and then."

"Yeah. It has." He took a step back. "Want a back rub?"

"Oh, yeah." Now they were back on solid ground. He'd offered the massage in the same tone of voice he always used, pre-kiss. As tense as Selena got when she flew, she had quickly learned to savor Eric's knot-dissolving backrubs. When she had thought he was Blair's boyfriend, she had always thought of Eric's touch as completely therapeutic. She would make herself think the same thing now.

He wrapped his hands around her shoulders so that his thumbs rested at the base of her neck and his fingertips touched the bare skin where her delicate silver chain rose and fell at the top of her breastbone.

He rubbed the pads of his thumbs in slow deliberate circles. The heat of his palms warmed her. The backrub drove the tension from her neck but failed to relax her as it usually did. Instead, she became aware of every shift of weight and every rustle of clothing between the two of them.

As his fingertips caressed her skin, she couldn't help the moan that escaped. With luck, Eric would think it meant the same as when he usually practiced his magic. In the rosy light, he wouldn't be able to see her flush. And as warm as his hands were, he wouldn't know how her temperature was rising.

She should tell him to stop, but willpower only went so far.

"Good?" His voice sounded sleepy and deep.

"Magic-hands Man."

A flash of light made her blink. Another flash, then another lit up the dusky sky. From her vantage point, she spotted a photographer setting up his tripod and aiming his camera in her direction. The Majestic always had a full galaxy of the rich and famous, should any star watchers care to ply their trade.

Had one of them just captured her on film? Chances were good that a number of cameras pointed to this balcony. Weeks ago, when Selena had reserved the room, she had assured the resort that Blair didn't mind pictures as long as the photographers respected her privacy. This was supposed to be Blair's publicity blitz. The Majestic always aimed to please.

That some industrious photographer might be taking blurry photos of her and Eric together sent a frisson of excitement down her spine.

Of course, her horny little imagination added in the idea about photos taken *en dishabille*. That idea sent bolts of lightning shooting through her. How did Eric feel about nudity and film?

Conversation, Selena. Polite, interesting conversation. That's what tonight was about, and tomorrow night and the night after that. Friendship. A meeting of the minds. A communal sharing of thoughts and beliefs.

That was a scary thought. What would happen if Eric learned what made her tick? Would he use it against her?

Why would he? Of course, he wouldn't. But reality slapped her in the face when she realized that was why she had never had a real lasting relationship before. Sex was easy. Trusting and sharing was hard. And voluntary vulnerability was even harder.

"Dinner smells great. What did you order for us?"

Eric held out her chair and she felt like a pampered princess. *"Chateaubriand* and *asparagus Béarnaise."*

193

His hand grazed her back as he adjusted the seating, and she felt more like a pampered princess than a paid assistant who played dress-up to help her boss out of a tight spot.

She swallowed and forced herself to think. "I thought you didn't like asparagus."

"No, but you do. I ordered *potatoes au gratin*, too. And *escargot*, just for fun."

She wrinkled her nose. "I don't eat bugs."

He laughed. "Are snails bugs?"

"Anything I usually sweep off the floor and throw outside is a bug."

"But these are special bugs. Just try them. The dessert will make up for it if you don't like them."

Eric pulled the cork on a bottle of merlot.

"That's your label, isn't it?"

"Yeah. I brought it with us in case the hotel didn't carry it." He poured with flair. "They don't. I've got to get the sales team in here."

Selena served herself a large helping of asparagus and put two tiny spears on Eric's plate. "I'm willing to eat insects if you'll eat your vegetables."

Eric eyed the asparagus like they were scum he'd scraped off the bottom of his shoe.

"Come on. They're not that bad. Trust me." Had she really said that? Had she really asked him to trust her? The second she said it, she wanted to clap her hand over her mouth. She and Eric had teased forever, but now, *Trust me* had taken on a much deeper meaning for her.

Eric leaned forward, capturing her focus with his sparkling eyes. "I trust you. Do you trust me?"

He held his fork toward her, snail entrapped on the tines.

"Fine. I'll go first."

At least she hadn't agreed to reciprocate. Not really. Only about vegetables and bugs.

The *escargot* was rich and wonderful. "Oh! Mmmm. So good!"

Eric looked into her eyes as if he were trying to read her mind. "Keep making noises like that and I'll order a dozen for every meal."

The intensity of his gaze made her hot. But then, everything about him tonight made her hot. She took a sip of her Merlot.

"I wonder what Blair is doing now?" Selena brought the conversation to a safe topic.

"Hopefully, she's napping. She looked awful. I don't think she's ever had hives before."

Selena pointed to the asparagus on Eric's plate. "Your turn."

Eric stuffed a whole spear in his mouth and chewed, obviously holding his breath. As soon as he swallowed, he gulped from his wine glass.

"Eww." His frown scrunched up his whole face. He had probably made the same face since he was three.

"It wasn't that bad, was it?"

"The things we do for love." The word *love* hung in the air.

Selena sawed off a piece of meat as if she were a lumberjack with a hacksaw. "Excellent beef."

"Much better than that green stuff." Eric finished up his potatoes.

The rest of the conversation centered on food, or the newest music video, or the fastest rollercoaster Selena had ever ridden and the rest of the Merlot.

By the time the bottle was emptied, the sky was dark. The new moon made the stars pop from the flat black night.

They hunched close over the candles to dip strawberries into melted chocolate and followed with a sip of champagne. The champagne tickled as it burst in Selena's mouth.

Dessert was full of moans and flicks of the tongue and innuendos. Selena blamed it on the bubbly. But the innuendos were fun and light, the sort of thing she and Eric had always shared.

Overall, she had a very fine dinner with a very good friend. Eric had now given her two blissful experiences to cherish.

"I had a lovely evening." Of course, that turned her thoughts to bed. By the way his eyes darkened, she had no doubt that Eric's thoughts had rushed down that same rail at breakneck speed. She couldn't see it, but she could sense a heart pounding drop just over the hill.

He was such a gentleman, he would offer to take the floor without even being prompted. There were plenty of pillows. He could pile them up on the floor and it would be softer than the mattress. The duvet from the bed would keep him warm enough as the night cooled down.

Of course, she wouldn't need the bed covering as she doubted her night would cool down at all.

As soon as she pushed her chair back, Eric did the same. Then he winced and sat back down.

"Damn it. My back." He rubbed his lower back. "I knew better when I lay on the floor to watch the game. Honey, would you mind getting me some Advil from my shaving kit?"

Honey? It was said as if they were an old, settled couple. Selena really liked the sound of it. What would it feel like to hear those endearments every day?

But her more immediate question was, if Eric's back was out, he couldn't sleep on the floor. She had no doubt that the staff would talk if they asked for a rollaway.

"Sure. I'll be right back."

She headed for the Advil, but stopped to take a long look at the bed on the way to the balcony.

They had to sleep sometime. No sense in putting it off any longer.

She took time out to dress in sweats for bed. They were too hot for the climate, but wearing less would have made her even hotter.

Emerging from the bathroom, she called, "Eric? Your turn."

He stood awkwardly in the bedroom doorway, as if awaiting her invitation.

It would be so simple, so easy. And he was different. She was sure of it. All she had to do was pull back the covers and pat the mattress beside her.

But then, when it was over, what would she lose?

She didn't want to find out.

Avoiding his eyes, she said, "We could put a pillow between us. The bed is plenty big enough for two. With the pillow between us, we won't even realize we're sharing.

"Besides, with the rich food and wine I had, I'll be sound asleep before you finish brushing his teeth."

"Uh, okay." He watched her use the king-sized pillow to separate the bed in half then turned off the light and climbed in. "Good night."

"Good night, Eric." She closed her eyes. Before she could count backwards from one hundred, her dreams were pushing into her wide-awake consciousness, showing her all she was denying herself.

She turned to face the wall. It was going to be a long night.

Midnight came and went. Eric lay in bed, miserable and aching. After much tossing and turning, Selena finally lay still on the other side of the massive bed, snoring gently. He wished he had kicked back more wine, or that he had ordered a bottle of whiskey to go along with the champagne.

CONNIE COX

Selena had been delighted with the bona fide bubbly from Champagne, especially when she realized how well it went with chocolate-dipped strawberries. She had oohed and aahed over the whole meal, raving about the *chateaubriand*, scarfing up the asparagus and giving the *escargot* a hesitant thumbs-up.

They had teased and laughed and talked and stood side-by-side, staring up into the stars. And he had thought, for just a little while, that it might be okay to enjoy himself, enjoy her, just for a little while since they both knew it would only be pretend.

Except his wouldn't be pretend.

He'd tried having a relationship once, going all the way and marrying her. And it had failed. He had failed. Like his father before him.

He wouldn't risk history repeating itself again.

But Selena wasn't like his ex-wife.

Despite the glitz and glamor, she was still Selena. She smiled the same when she ate snails from his fork. She moaned the same when he rubbed circles under her shoulder blades. She moved the same, even under her heavy sweats.

No, Selena wasn't anything like the little starlet who'd wanted his money and his influence and nothing else.

She hadn't even wanted to accept his backrub until he convinced her that it would give him as much pleasure as her.

And it had.

His fingers twitched even now as he remembered the feel of her shoulder blades as he rubbed her bare back. He might have relieved her tension, but now he got it back tenfold. He felt like a rubber band stretched on the verge of breaking.

But her neck to ankle sweats were a big clue about how far she wanted to go.

What happened to the woman he'd kissed last night?

No, he didn't need to think about that kiss.

He needed to get rid of this throbbing ache of a tent pole before he burst.

With great care, he rolled out of bed.

"Eric?" Her sleepy voice almost cured him of his pain prematurely.

"Bathroom."

CHAPTER NINE

The next morning, Selena awoke grumpy and disgruntled. She should have been feeling proud of her willpower to want more than just sex. Instead, all she felt this morning was horny and miserable. She had never been so frustrated in her life. And it was all her own doing.

What was she thinking, inviting Eric to sleep in the same bed with her?

If he had tempted her, just a little, her resolve would have melted completely away.

Thinking of him as her platonic friend wasn't so easy knowing Blair wouldn't mind at all if they became something more.

Or course, realistically, Eric *did* have some say in the matter. If she did offer something more than friendship, he could turn her down.

Would he?

What did she want?

Selena ran her hands through what was left of her hair and took a deep breath.

What she really wanted was a real relationship with a man she trusted. A man she was not only attracted to sexually, but also mentally. A man who would be her best friend as well as her lover.

What she wanted was Eric. More than just want as eye candy. But want with a need, a desire which went beyond the physical to a place deep inside her that wanted to be breached, wanted to be touched and protected by him, and wanted him to want her in the same way.

The realization made her legs shake so hard, she plopped down on the concrete-hard sofa and put her head down between her knees.

No. She couldn't want him that way. She couldn't want anyone that way. That level of emotion took trust. Eating *escargot* was one thing, but letting another person get that far inside her head or her heart were entirely different things.

She was not a masochist. She didn't go around doing things she knew would eventually end in pain. Never again—and her first time in love came nowhere close to where she wanted this time to go. In love? No. Not going to happen.

She sat up just as Eric wandered into the sitting area, looking like he'd had the worst night of his life. Stubble peppered his jaw line. Crevasses bracketed his mouth. And his bloodshot eyes looked like he had just viewed his own personal hell.

"Morning." He grunted to her.

"Morning. She echoed back, and swept her hand toward the room service tray they had ordered the night before. He looked so sexy with his hair sticking up all over and pillow creases in his cheeks and his eyes heavy and blinking. And there went her wants again.

She wanted to know what he dreamed at night to make him smile and mumble in his sleep. She wanted to smooth down his hair, run her fingers across his cheeks and kiss his eyes into awareness.

Instead, she clenched her fists. Not going to happen.

They were friends. She wouldn't deny that. Friends *without* benefits, but friends, nevertheless.

Would friendship satisfy her needs? More than casual, more than flirty fun, but true, close friendship? The kind of close friendship Eric had with Blair.

That deep empty place inside her begged for more.

Friendship would be enough—more than enough. More than she had with anyone else on the planet.

She could let that happen.

Maybe even encourage that to happen.

Her restlessness backed off the slightest of degrees at the thought of spending quality time building her friendship with Eric.

Safely, silently, they each hid behind a newspaper section as they ate breakfast. He was a juice man and she was a diet Coke kind of girl, but they both preferred bagels to toast and sausage to bacon.

Their paper-reading styles differed but they worked it out. As she would finish one section of the paper, still perfectly smooth and folded correctly, she handed it off to him.

Eric wasn't quite so neat. He crumpled, twisted and wadded as he read. But he was considerate enough to wait until she had finished. Except for the testy silence, it was as if they had shared breakfast for years. Then again, maybe irritability would have been their *fiber de jour* if they had been eating breakfast together for a few decades.

After an extremely quiet hour, Eric pushed away from the table. "I think I'll take a shower, then we can see what's on TV." His tone was loud, pseudo-cheerful and damned grating.

Selena put down the last section of the paper. She didn't think she could stand to have the TV blaring between them. How would she strike up a meaningful conversation while hysterical people jumped up and down trying to win go-carts and cans of peas from overly-groomed game show hosts?

Then genius struck. If she could just get Eric out of the room for a while....

"You mentioned wanting to play golf. It looks like a beautiful morning for it. I won't pout too much about being stuck here all by myself, as long as you keep me company this afternoon."

Eric breathed an unflattering sigh of relief. "Okay. Great. I'll call for a tee time and give you a little space."

A quick call to the concierge had tee time secured.

Eric rubbed his hand through his grubby hair, stretched and yawned. "Shower time."

He gulped the rest of his juice then practically bounced out of the room, anxious to get on with his day.

As soon as she heard the bathroom door close, she scribbled a note and stuck it on top of their dirty dishes, then set the tray outside for the clean-up crew.

While Eric was out chasing little dimpled balls, Selena pampered herself with another long soak, gave herself a pedicure and answered email on her laptop. Shortly before noon, the maintenance man began disabling the big screen in the sitting area while she stayed hidden in the bedroom, flipping channels on the smaller television tucked into the armoire.

On the concierge's channel, she discovered that she could use the TV to email the staff with any needs she had, just like text messaging.

That solved the communication problem, since calling them on the phone was out of the question. New Mexico had left too deep a stamp on Selena's speech pattern to copy Blair's California Valley Girl accent, and email was easier than notes smuggled out on food trays.

The maintenance man must think I'm crazy—uh, Blair's crazy. What would he tell the nightshift about her request written on a breakfast napkin? But then, the Majestic was used to hosting celebrities. He had probably complied with requests a lot more eccentric than hers. At least she hadn't asked him to hand-sort her M&Ms by color, like her least favorite spoiled heiress did.

What was taking that maintenance man so long? She watched the clock wondering how long Eric's game would last. Bad things could happen if Eric walked in on the maintenance guy taking parts off the TV. Finally, she heard the man pack up his tools and leave.

Being restricted to one room, not matter how luxurious, had quickly turned cloying.

She sent a message for the maids asking them to forgo the housecleaning and leave clean towels, along with a stack of board games, in the sitting room.

As Selena hid out of sight in the bedroom, the staff brought lunch, an uninspired sandwich from the in-house grill and, much more exciting, the tools to kick off her *getting to know Eric better* plan.

The cardboard boxes of the board games looked well used. But then, who really cared if Scrabble had all the letters intact as long as a friendly match led to conversation?

By mid-afternoon, Selena had started to wonder if Eric would ever return. Boredom had her crawling into their unmade bed to nap.

She lay her head on a pillow and realized it was the one Eric had used. His wonderful, distinctive scent made her more restless and she threw the pillow onto the floor but the sheets still held his smell. After flopping, twisting and sprawling, Selena gave up on the napping idea.

She was just about to read through the room service menu again when she heard the door rattle.

"Honey, I'm home."

She knew he joked, but for half a second she wished he didn't. "How was your game?"

"I think the golf pro was embarrassed to be seen with me. When I told him I wanted beginner instructions, he didn't understand that I wasn't kidding." He rubbed his shoulder. "I'm going to be sore in the morning."

He lay down a handful of gossip rags. "We made the inside pages of a couple of local papers. Not the national ones, though."

"Maybe tonight."

"Maybe so." He took off his shoes, stared at the settee and sat in one of the equally uncomfortable wing chairs. "Wonder what's on TV." He reached for the remote control and pointed it at the television.

Selena pretended not to hear as she studied their blurry likeness in one of the papers.

Eric slapped the back of the remote. "Batteries must be weak. I'll call Maintenance."

"I already did. It will take a while to fix. Parts or something? So I asked them to bring up a bunch of board games for us."

"Is that b-o-r-e-d or b-o-a-r-d?" He walked up to the television and clicked again.

"Room service brought a couple of different ones. Pick one."

"You'd think, as much as this suite costs, they could fix our TV." Disgusted, Eric finally stopped clicking the remote at the screen and glanced at the stack of boxes on the coffee table. With a defeated air, he lay the remote down next to the boxes. "You'll have to teach me. I've never played any of them."

"You're kidding. These are classics."

"Nope. I was an only child, remember?"

"Yeah, me, too. But my mom and I would play for hours. One summer, we had a Monopoly marathon that ran for weeks. We would talk and talk." Selena paused. "They're some of the best memories I have."

He looked deep into her eyes, like he was trying to find a hidden message. His own eyes became soft and kind. She wanted to reach for him and feel that tenderness in his touch but that would be crossing the friend barrier. Not going to happen. Friendship was enough—more than enough. Regardless of how hard she tried to push it back, the thought flitted through her mind, *But what if there could be more?*

From the way Eric absently fingered the remote control, nothing even close to Selena's thoughts was flitting through his mind.

"A board game marathon sounds like fun." Eric pulled the Monopoly box from the bottom. "Let's play."

"Let's play," she echoed, determined to think only about playing with dice and fake money.

Selena set up the board and explained the rules and Eric listened intently, taking them all in and asking questions that showed he understood the strategy behind the game. Until now, she'd never realized how competitive he was.

They moved their pewter dog and top hat pieces around the board and they talked about people they knew, people they didn't know and, finally about themselves.

As Selena listened to Eric's childhood stories of traveling with his father, she realized he had spent his childhood among adults. He'd had everything he wanted but friends. No wonder he was such a social animal now.

Eric rolled the dice. "After Mom left, Dad kept me close. He wanted to make sure I didn't feel abandoned. Although he's never said an unkind word about my mother, I'm fairly certain that's the way he felt."

He landed on the Electric Company and bought it. "So he took me on the road with him whenever a play opened. Of course, he wrote when he wasn't setting up a production. Sitting in a hotel room with your father typing away for hours can be fairly dull. The night my dad won his Emmy, the concierge at the Ritz-Carlton taught me to play Five-card stud to keep me from pushing all the buttons on the elevators again."

He was such an outgoing kind of guy, sharing the life of his solitary screenwriter-producer-director father must have been so dull it was painful.

"What about school?"

"Home-schooled, or schooled on the set with the underage actors. Most of them are adults in kids' bodies, though. All serious and rushing through their work so they can get back to the set. I had never even been in a classroom until college."

Even the time spent on his grandmother's estate had been spent in isolation. He hadn't even played team sports since he couldn't be sure to finish out a season. His only interaction had been enrolment in an occasional extracurricular class like dance or martial arts when he was home in Sonoma.

The more he talked, the more she realized how alike they were. They had the same view on politics, on talk show hosts and even on philosophy, although her views were more cynical than his.

Eric liked to analyze. He liked to take people apart and guess what made them tick. His depth of insight astounded her and she realized that he was brilliant in his own particular way. But, he admitted, he couldn't figure out those closest to him.

As he told her of his parents' divorce he was obviously still puzzled about why. He had a half-brother in France where his mother lived with his stepfather. Stepdad was a great guy, an art broker, and treated his mother like a beloved queen. Eric visited every now and then, but kept the visits short.

"I always feel like a guest, someone to be entertained and then sent on my way."

"You didn't go over for summers?"

"Mom didn't settle down until my brother was born. Before that, she did some stage acting, then got into interior decorating and fashion consulting. She never knew where she'd be from day to day. It would have been difficult."

Selena heard the hurt in Eric's words even though the tone of his voice was matter-of-fact.

She wanted to hold him in her arms and make it all better. Instead, she paid the rent for landing on one of his properties. He didn't even notice the yellow and pink bills she lay on his side of the table.

"How old is your brother?"

"Thirteen." He passed up the chance to buy the fourth railroad to go with his other three. "I was offered an apprenticeship to study with one of the great vineyards in France but I turned it down. Maybe that would have made things different. I might have even gotten to know my half-brother. But what-ifs are fairly useless, aren't they?"

"Why didn't you go?"

"My marriage was shaky at the time and we were trying to work things out."

Marriage? Before she could decide to probe or not, Eric asked, "What about your life's history? Any skeletons in your closet?"

Selena rolled the dice and knocked Eric's dog off the table. "Sorry."

She dove under the table, took an extra second for a deep breath, then emerged sunny and smiling.

She told him the basics. Daughter of a single mom. Not much money but lots of love. Her mother had worked at a local amusement park to support them both. Selena didn't mention the side jobs her mom took, the jobs that made the real money that paid the trailer rent and the electric bill.

Instead, she turned the conversation to wine, asking about his plans for Walking Hill.

His eyes sparkled as he talked of vertical farming and the ecosystem.

When Selena landed on Atlantic, she told him about the exhilaration she felt when she rode her first grownup roller coaster.

"The thrill has never faded. After that first drop, I feel like I'm bigger and braver than anyone else in the world. Like the world can't hold me down. And then, when it's all over, it's like I've not only survived, but laughed in the face of fear. I feel so tingly, so alive."

"Why do you insist on riding alone?"

"Because it's all illusion, of course. Someone else would spoil it." Selena used her Get Out of Jail Free card. "Someone else would say something practical like, 'This has been tested a thousand times. Up and down and around, what's the big deal'. Or they might whine the whole way about too fast, too high, too scary. Then I would have to destroy the illusion myself to calm them down and take care of them. No, thank you. Solo is the only way to ride a roller coaster." She rolled the dice, pulled the Go To Jail card and plopped her top hat behind bars.

Eric rolled and landed on Baltic Avenue. He handed her pink and blue money and she handed him the cardboard deed. "So you ride alone so no one can mess it up for you?"

"Yeah. When I've been standing in line forever, I don't want to be disappointed when it's finally my turn."

"But what if someone enjoyed the ride as much as you did? Wouldn't it be more fun to share?"

"Why take the chance when I know I'll have a blast all by myself?" Selena turned on a lamp. "The afternoon has gone by quickly. Do you want to continue this tomorrow? It's time to get ready for our game of balcony charades?"

Eric looked shocked, then sheepish. "I forgot about our mission. By all means, let us dress for our performance. I'll order dinner while you change."

Selena slipped into her dress and heels, forgoing the theatrical makeup she'd applied last night. Tonight, she wanted Eric to see *her* behind the Blair hair.

She wanted Eric to know her, to understand what made her tick, to feel a connection with her like she was beginning to feel with him. Was that close friendship?

How could it happen so fast? A small voice whispered that it had been there all along. She just didn't want to see it.

She slipped into a simple cocktail dress and heels dyed to match. The peach-colored chiffon had thin spaghetti straps and a short, full skirt.

From the sitting room, she could hear Eric still ordering their dinner.

She glided into the sitting room and pirouetted.

"Wow. Oh, wow." Eric drawled, thick and deep. "No, not you," he said into the phone, "although I'm sure the soufflé will be very nice."

He hung up the phone, missed the coffee table and let the receiver fall to the floor instead.

Selena held her arms out for inspection. "You like?"

"Yeah, I like." He stood motionless until Selena prompted, "Go change."

Eric left the room, walking backward to delay having to tear his gaze from Selena.

Selena couldn't stop smiling. It felt good to be admired.

Eric took longer with his dressing than she had. His shower seemed to last forever. But Selena was fast learning that Eric liked long showers. Just like she learned that he was fastidious with his food orders and sloppy about leaving his shoes wherever he took them off.

When she thought of Eric taking off his clothes, the room became hot and stuffy. Selena checked the fading sunset and deemed it safe to step out onto the balcony.

Immediately, flashes began popping from below. The Majestic's staff and Blair's PR rep were doing a fine job.

Eric joined her, looking damned fine in his tux.

By the way he stared, Eric seemed to like the thigh-high view as the early evening breeze blew the filmy chiffon.

As soon as he came beside her, the ground beneath them flickered with more flashes, like lightning bugs on steroids.

Eric quirked his mouth sarcastically. "Think the paparazzi are catching all this?"

"Blair will be pleased."

"Screw Blair." Eric looked embarrassed at his outburst. "It's getting damned irritating. Photographers even tried to invade the golf course this morning. But security did their thing and we all played in peace."

"I'm sorry this is putting you out so much. I know you're only doing this out of friendship." *And this is how easily friendship can end*, Selena added to herself. *One regretted promise and it's all over.*

Eric took a deep breath, put his arm around Selena's shoulder and led her to the balcony rail. "I would do it all again, a thousand times over, for the woman I care about so deeply."

Selena pulled away to look into his eyes, surprised at his impassioned confession. "Blair is special, isn't she?" She couldn't help feel sorry for both of them for the unrequited infatuation in his voice.

His eyes turned sad as he looked back at her.

She reached to straighten his tie, just so she could touch his cheek.

He caught her hand and lifted her fingers to his lips.

Selena was fairly certain the cameras couldn't pick up the details at this distance, but she couldn't bring herself to point out this fact to Eric. Instead, she enjoyed the moment, wishing she wasn't pretending to be someone else.

As the night grew darker, the oversized, artificial lightning bug flashes went away. It was hard to remember that some intrepid photographer might be using infrared for night shots.

Room service arrived, forcing Selena to scurry into the bedroom and hid behind the door until they set up the meal and left. The break gave herself a chance to pull back and remember that this was all a farce. But Selena firmly pushed logic to the back of her thoughts.

The meal was exquisite. Not just the food but also the conversation. Classic piano played softly from hidden speakers as they clinked glasses and proposed silly toasts.

"To the best moonbeam." Eric lifted his glass high.

Selena copied him and said, "I'll drink to that."

Then, "To that bright twinkling star up there." She had to hold Eric's hand and guide his finger so he would know exactly which one.

"Here, here." He toasted with his free hand, but not breaking free of her hold.

Over dessert, they continued to explore each other like they had done during their monopoly game. But under the cover her darkness, Selena found secrets so much easier to divulge.

Eric asked about her dreams and her aspirations. She found herself telling him about wanting to understand the magic of rollercoasters, the g-forces, the vectors and the speed that made her heart race. When he didn't laugh or tell her that only the smartest people could design coasters, she told him more.

She told him about how she had hidden her math scores because her mother had said that men didn't like to be shown up by smart women, and how frustrated she had felt. She told him how she was the first person in her family to graduate from high school and how proud her grandmother had been and about how she had received a scholarship to the state college, but didn't have enough money to live on and didn't know how to apply for student loans until the deadline had passed.

She forgot they were posing for the cameras when she volunteered to rub his stiffening back.

The moans he made when she kneaded his tight shoulder blades made her wonder what noises he made during foreplay. He took off his jacket, then untucked his shirt so she could get better friction.

When her fingertips touched the bare skin under his shirt, her palms startled tingling. She had to jerk her hands away as the tingle traveled down her arms like an electric shock. But she wasn't quick enough. The prickle spread across her breasts, making them so sensitive that they ached for Eric's touch.

Your rules, Selena. Keep them or break them? A spotlight pinned them from below, reminding her that this was all an illusion. She hugged herself instead.

Of course, Eric noticed. "Cold?"

"No. Just ready to go inside."

For the next three days, they followed the same routine. Breakfast. Golf for Eric. Mindless net surfing, room service ordering and television watching for Selena. Then Monopoly and conversation.

They discussed politics, philosophy, and even religion. No subject was taboo as long as it was academic. Each time the conversation turned personal, Selena would guide it back to generalities.

Each evening, their balcony performance of a couple in love, or at least in lust, was convincing enough to garner the press they needed.

Eric played his part well, so well it confused Selena. He would lean toward her over the table as they ate and stand with his arm around her as they studied the moon.

Sometimes, it seemed he forgot it was all a game and he would whisper tender words to her, telling her how beautiful she was, how special she was, how lucky a man would be if she were in his life. When she rested her hand on the railing, he would cover her hand with his own. His touch would make her warm inside.

Then he would give her a heated glance and that warmth would turn to fire and need.

Once, as he rubbed his thumb across her palm at dinner, she reminded him that the photographers couldn't see his provocative gesture. He was staying in character, had been his answer. She was hoping for something else. Instead she got a reminder that her world was a stage and she was merely a well-paid actress.

That would teach her. If she wasn't prepared for the truth, she shouldn't ask.

And she would hurt. Knowing that this was all just a slice out of time, a fairy tale that was never meant to last, gave her an ache so bad she would have to fight back the tears.

On the fourth day, somewhere between Boardwalk and bankruptcy, she asked Eric about his first wife.

He paused long enough that Selena was about to apologize for prying, then he said, "I was nineteen and loving every minute of college life but hating each writing class I signed up for. But screenwriting was the only life I knew. Emily was five years older, an actress on the verge of breaking through. She showed me a bigger life. Parties and coffee houses and hanging out with friends for the fun of it. She told me I was fascinating and my naiveté was refreshingly fun. I thought I had found the perfect woman. I introduced her to my mother and they became fast friends."

Eric rolled the dice and landed on Park Place. He shelled out the money for a hotel even though it took his last dollar. "They still are."

Selena didn't bother to tell Eric he had miscounted and should have landed on her property instead. She had never seen his eyes this clouded before.

He rolled the dice again. A pair of ones. Snake eyes. "Everyone said we were perfect for each other. Afterward, I realized that 'everyone' had been her tight clique of friends who thought that the son of a brilliant playwright might introduce them to the right people.

"And I did.

"Emily loved the glamour, the fast pace, the sparkling nights and the invitations that my dad's reputation bought us. I have to admit, I loved it, too."

Eric passed Go and Selena handed him two hundred in Monopoly money. "Sure, I was a partying kind of guy, but I had started to feel like Emily's meal ticket instead of her husband. Her friends called me her little rich boy to my face. She thought it was funny.

"Eventually, I just wanted to wake up to the smell of green leaves growing and the feel of mist in the mornings. I wanted to get my hands dirty and to watch the grapes grow full after a rainstorm. I missed the quiet of the sunsets. I missed the calmness of the land.

"The first tasting of a new vintage wine held more excitement than the premiere of any movie I had ever attended. It didn't help that I barely passed English Lit. Too many late nights and hangovers on exam day."

Selena pulled a card and counted out her penalty for the community chest fund. "It sounds like you were trying to flunk out."

Eric looked startled. "You know, I think you're right. I'd never thought of that before." He rolled the dice and knocked his dog off the table. When he bent to retrieve it, he ran his hand along Selena's shin.

Accident? Maybe. Selena hoped not.

Selena would have been content to leave the conversation unfinished. After all, they both had histories. Did she really want to share?

Apparently, Eric did, because he kept talking. "After the wedding, we moved to the vineyard. On reflection, the move was totally selfish on my part.

"Emily didn't like the isolation. The breezy afternoons sitting on the veranda, the long expanses of silence tortured her instead of soothed her. She claimed the boredom drove her to do coke."

Selena pinned him with her stare. "Nobody makes another person take drugs." He needed to understand. "It's not your fault."

"Maybe." He didn't believe her. "I can't remember even taking Emily's feelings into consideration. I was so self-centered then."

Selena thought about how considerate he was to her. He had must have changed a lot in the last eight years. But, then, so had she.

"Finally, Emily convinced me that the vineyard was the source of all her problems. So we moved back to the city. I re-enrolled in college and took whatever classes I felt like taking. They ended up being agriculture and business classes. Emily was comfortable in the city. I was comfortable in school. But we weren't comfortable with each other."

The inevitable, Selena thought. But she didn't say it. Eric still saw his failed marriage as his fault, instead of a fault of the universe. Selena acknowledged that there might be a good long lasting relationship or two out there, but she had never seen one.

Eric looked sheepish. "I'm sorry. I didn't mean to spill all this."

Selena heard insecurity in Eric's voice, as if he worried that she judged him. She knew that worry too well. And she was the last person who should be passing judgment on anyone else. "You're a good man, Eric. Sometimes, things just don't work out between two people." She could have added 'most of the time', but Eric didn't need her cynicism.

Because she sensed he needed to finish his confession, she asked, "Then what happened?"

"Then there was Blair." He said it defiantly, as if he expected her to condemn him on the spot. "She was in a bad place at a bad time and, well, I intervened."

Selena wanted to know more, but she respected his privacy and didn't ask for details. Maybe someday....

She caught herself. Someday? Like in the future? This was all pretend. She and Eric didn't have a future. Did they?

Selena had had too much time on her hands. Too much time to examine her life. Too much time to realize that Eric was different, not like all the other guys she had dated. Every evening she felt closer and closer to him. She might even love him. And he might love her back. Character acting be damned.

Each time she came to that conclusion, she waited for the familiar panicked feeling to overwhelm her, to bring her to her senses as it brought her to her knees. But loving Eric wasn't scary at all. It was warm and safe and comforting. And it made her feel wanted. She'd never felt wanted before.

By unspoken agreement, they skipped the balcony farce and went to bed early. She could tell by his breathing that Eric wasn't sleep. Neither was she.

She started talking. Why she picked now, why she picked him, she didn't know. Maybe it had to do with the darkness. In the dark, she didn't have to watch his face, didn't have to see the disgust or the pity. She told him about her mother's after-hours job, the one that kept her out all night and had her drinking her breakfast while she tried to wash off the odors of sweating men.

The job that had kept Selena fed and clothed.

She even told Eric how the kids at school had taught her what the world's oldest profession had been by writing it all over her mother's car and how, to this day, she couldn't say the words they had spray painted in vivid red and pink.

And she told him how she had to struggle to keep herself from following down her mother's path.

She wanted so badly to roll over into his arms, to feel his strength around her, to let him soothe the little girl she'd been.

Eric grabbed the pillow that separated them and threw it to the floor. He opened up his arms and she lay against him, her head on his shoulder. She had never felt this safe in her whole life.

Eric hadn't judged. Instead, he'd said good things about her mother's strength and about her valiant struggle to raise her daughter as best she could. He's also said good things about Selena about how smart and brave she was for making her own way in the world.

And Selena believed him.

CHAPTER TEN

The Cabo San Lucas sunshine warmed the oil that Dominic poured onto Blair's bare back. Music floated from the open glass doors into the tiny, private walled courtyard that separated their beach house from the other vacation homes along the shoreline.

Dominic massaged the tension from her lower back as he rubbed in the sunscreen oil. "You don't want to burn while erasing those nasty tan lines, now do you?"

"Tan lines bad. Burnt butt worse." She giggled as he slathered an extra coat across her bare bottom. She felt great, as if the hives had never taken over her body. It was amazing what a little R&R and a lot of good sex could do to heal a woman. "You ended up with a nice even all-over golden-brown. Next time, I think I'll surf without a swimsuit, like you did yesterday."

Dominic's hand slowed as poured more oil onto her back. "I told you, it was that pesky mermaid that yanked it off. Then she forced herself on me."

"I have the story straight from the pesky mermaid's mouth. She was grateful she could outswim you. Otherwise, you would have stripped off her swimsuit bottom just like she stripped yours. She wouldn't have liked to paddle back to shore on her board, lying on her stomach like you did." Blair looked back at him over her shoulder. "I—uh—she would have missed that killer wave."

"That was a pretty ride, sweetie, even if I had to watch from the safety of your beach towel." Dominic traced lazy figure eights around the dimples in her lower back, then slid his fingers down to curve around the fullness of her bottom. "From now on, I'll be your panties."

"You're a perfect fit."

"Like a hand to a glove?" He kept his fingers sliding until his middle finger found the perfect place to make her squirm.

She lifted her hips to give him more room to play.

With a single flick, he had her so hot that he teased out liquid sunshine. "Do you like this?"

"Yesssssss."

"Do you want me to stop?"

"Noooooooo."

Tension coiled. She arched her back, driving his finger deeper as his hand cupped her. His other hand splayed across her bottom with his strong, callused trigger finger at the hypersensitive end of the tailbone. She felt deliciously trapped between those two strong hands as he worked them in rhythm to caress her.

"Good?" His voice was deep and sure with pride.

"You know it is." She rocked herself against his tempo, throbbing with each beat.

"How about this?" He eased into her, his hard body covering her with possession.

"Ummmphh." Her powers of speech deserted her.

Everything she thought or felt whirled to become one tight all-consuming circle of need that promised salvation with just...

One...

More...

Stroke...

YES!

Her world pulsed around her in a swirl of sound and color and aroma, each blending into the other. She didn't even recognize her own voice as it blended into his.

Ecstasy forced out a moan that came from an ocean so deep within her it had never before surfaced.

Dom's own rumble of release reverberated into that same deep ocean, filling her with a completeness she'd never felt before.

Down, down she fell into the bottomless sea as wave after wave broke over her. Finally, eons later, the waves became gentle swells that pushed her to shore, sleepy and sated.

Dom rolled onto his side and she rolled to face him, blinking heavy lids to focus on his face. His gentle, relaxed smile told her all she needed to know. With a deep sigh, she closed her eyes and gave into blissful stupor.

Time passed by unheeded until Dom pulled a beach towel over her. She realized the air had become chilled with the approaching sunset and her skin was pebbling under the temperature drop.

"Hungry?" she asked.

"I could eat." He traced the pattern of the beach towel over her breasts. "What are you in the mood for?"

She squinted against the setting sun and tried to think beyond the moment.

Her cell phone mewed like a kitten, interrupting her scattered thoughts. A photo of Selena popped up on the display to accompany the kitten-meow ring.

She pushed away Dominic's roving hand so she could concentrate enough to answer with a semblance of coherence. "Hey, Selena. What's up?"

"Just calling to check on you." Selena's voice sounded strained and fake-cheerful.

"I'm doing much better. Dominic's got me on a strict schedule of R&R, so I've been indulging in lots of naps." She giggled as Dom nibbled her neck.

"You sound breathless. You're taking your antihistamine, aren't you?"

"Yup." She rubbed her foot against Dominic's hairy leg, forgetting whatever else she had intended to say.

"How much longer, do you think?" Selena sounded a bit on the grumpy side. "Not that I'm rushing you or anything. But a hotel suite, no matter how beautiful and spacious, starts shrinking after four days."

Blair sat up. "Selena, I am so sorry. I'm getting better as fast as I can."

Dominic leaned in close to share the phone. "Hey, Selena."

"Hey, Dom. Taking care of our girl?" Selena's cheerfulness definitely sounded forced.

"You bet."

Blair's stomach growled. How could she end this conversation without offending Selena? "I saw a great shot of you and Eric on the veranda. If I hadn't known better, I would have thought you were me."

"Um-hmm." Selena didn't sound placated. "Eric is playing a lot of golf. I've watched TV until my eyes hurt. I've Googled everyone and everything I can think of. Want to know how many fractions of an inch hair grows in a month on the average woman?"

Dominic spoke into the phone. "You've always wanted to learn to knit, right? You could always order a video and supplies. Just call the concierge and have whatever you want delivered."

Blair elbowed him and mouthed, *That's stupid.*

"Yeah, I guess. Thanks, Dom." By Selena's tone, she thought it was stupid, too, but was too polite to say so.

He shrugged at Blair. "Well, it was great to hear from you, Selena. We'd better go so I can get a good meal down Blair then get her into bed."

Blair rolled her eyes at his blatantness. Dom was such a carefree kid when they were alone, so different from when he was on guard.

"Okay. Bye, then." Selena sounded pitiful. "Get well soon, Blair."

Blair broke the connection. Poor Selena, all by her lonesome. What was Eric doing? He better not be blowing this opportunity.

Eric's phone rang in midstroke. His masterful attempt to reach the green failed miserably as his ball dribbled off the tee. But the wasted shot wasn't as bad as the barbed looks and raised hackles directed his way from the foursome waiting at the tee off box.

He dropped his club and fumbled for his phone as a tinny version of Blair's Men, Monsters and Muscles chirped from his hip.

The pro he had hired for the last three days tried to show his disapproval without pissing off the worst golfer but biggest tipper that had come through the resort in two years.

"Hold on, Blair."

At the name Blair, the two younger of the foursome raised brows and stood down. They whispered to the older couple who shook their heads and continued to glare.

Eric held the phone away from his mouth. "Why don't you play through?"

He didn't know if he was breaking golf etiquette or not, but at least they let him escape.

He walked over to his cart, his pro trailing behind him, bringing his forgotten club.

"What's up? Are you all right?" Eric popped open the tab to a Coke and the oldest of the foursome stared back at him. He raised it in a toast and swallowed back a gulp.

"I'm getting better all the time." She sounded angry.

Uh-oh. Had it been the cosmetic surgery rumor that one of the tabloids ran yesterday? At least no one had run a drug rehab story yet. Eric could never figure out why the media and the public always assumed drugs and never a sore throat or common cold.

"That's good to hear. Are you ready to end this—
" He looked over at the pro who was diligently
scraping mud off the club faces an arm's length
away. "—this relationship?"

Let the tabloids get hold of that one.

"Selena called. She's bored stiff. What's the deal?
You've been fascinated with her ever since you met
her. You've got the perfect setup, Eric and you're
blowing it."

Eric scowled into the phone then cast a sharp
glance at the pro.

Whispering, he said, "I've done a hell of a lot for
you in the past few days and now you're
haranguing me?"

"Eric, sweetie, what are best friends for if not to
tell you when you're screwing up." She paused,
then said, "You've got a sharp edge to your voice.
I'm thinking it's not because you're screwing up, it's
because you're not screwing at all."

With a smirk very visible to the pro, he said, "It's
only platonic, honey. She's not even interested in
anything else."

"Selena hasn't done anything to show she's
interested? Eric, that's hard to believe."

"Nope. Nothing." He didn't count the midnight
kiss, before this farce even got started. Nor did he

count waking up this morning to have her long, strong leg thrown over his. She was asleep and didn't even know she'd done it. He should be cast in bronze for his chivalry. In fact, he'd been so hard after he untangled himself that he thought he *had* been encased in bronze and had to act with great gentleness to answer his early morning wakeup call.

"She tells me she's been stuck in that room for over three days now."

"We all knew that was the way this was going to work when we started it." Eric was very aware of the curiosity of the golf pro, so he kept his voice lowered even when he wanted to say more.

"You've been out and about, playing while she's stuck by herself." Blair's face must be pinched tight to match the scolding tone of her voice.

"She hasn't been totally neglected. We've dined together, watched TV together, talked, you know, friend stuff." And it had been friend stuff. They had talked about their childhoods, their parents, even about their dreams. Where he and Selena had been casual friends once, now they were fast developing a deep friendship. The potential had been there ever since their first meeting, they only had to give themselves a chance.

He realized Blair had been droning on all this time. "Dom says it's because you've never had to put the moves on a woman before. The women have always thrown themselves at you."

"You've been talking to Dom about me?" That didn't sit well.

"You don't talk to Selena about me?" She had him there. He and Selena had psychoanalyzed Blair, Dominic and Allan and all their other mutual acquaintances with a thoroughness that would have made Jung proud. Eric had always been fascinated with what made people tick—a legacy from his screenwriter-director father, no doubt. But he'd never been able to share his armchair psychology philosophies with anyone he'd ever known, even Blair. Until Selena.

With her, he felt he could share anything that popped into his head.

"Eric? Are you even listening to me?"

"I'm listening." Eric glared at the pro who suddenly found something very interesting to explore in the bushes several yards away. It was about damned time.

"Well, what do you think?"

Uh-oh, what had he missed. "About what?"

"About taking her on your boat for a day or two, let her enjoy the sunshine and fresh air. It's done me a world of good."

"I think you shouldn't be trying to tell me what to do."

"Apparently someone needs to. Hold on." She covered the mouthpiece but not before he heard her say something about idiot men. "I've got to go. Still friends?"

"Yeah, I guess." He didn't care that it sounded sulky.

But the outing on the boat wasn't really a bad idea. He called over the pro. "Sorry, I've got to cut this game short." He was fairly certain it was a big golf no-no to leave before he finished, but, hey, he was a grape grower, not a little dimpled ball chaser. What did he care?

They drove back to the clubhouse and he paid the pro enough to soothe any golf etiquette affront he could have caused, then made a few quick phone calls before he headed up to the room.

Selena stared down at the wad of yarn that trapped her wrists and tangled around her ankles. What was supposed to be relaxing about this? She shook out of the knotted mess and wandered around her gilded cage wondering what to do next. Even mentally adding up the growing balance in her savings account couldn't lift her spirits.

Last night, when she had fallen asleep in his arms, Eric had held her, just held her, and hadn't expected anything in return.

This morning, she thought she would be embarrassed about her midnight confessions. She expected to regret her unrestricted outpourings. But she didn't. Instead, she felt light and happy. She felt as if she'd just finished the most terrifying roller coaster ride of her life and not only lived through it but learned she had wings and could fly after all.

And she felt that she wanted more from Eric. More than friendship. More than a week out of time. *More*.

He had called her brave. Was she?

A restlessness took hold of her and the walls seemed to close in. This charade for Blair was doing a number on her. Who would have thought that doing nothing could be so hard? Maybe some exercise to work off the excess energy.

She fired up her laptop and sat down to write her latest email to the front desk.

The first time she emailed them, she'd felt silly. But Blair's voice was so distinctive, so unlike hers, that she couldn't call them, and using the concierge screen and the channel changer on the bedroom TV had really cramped her thumbs.

Her first request had been for books, magazines and crossword puzzles along with a standing order for the maids to come in, drop off the loot and leave.

Selena had overheard the maids when they delivered her requests.

Their whispers carried louder than they realized, but then she had been listening hard, with her ear pressed to the door. They knew about the note to the maintenance man to put the big screen out of commission, too. Blair's reputation as an eccentric had begun.

The initial instructions to forgo cleaning the bathroom, to leave clean sheets outside the bedroom door and never to enter the bedroom had left them wondering about plastic surgery or detox. Apparently, many celebrities came to the Majestic to recover.

Feeling a bit snarky yesterday afternoon, Selena had requested publications about boob lift recovery. In less than half an hour, the staff had produced everything from medical journals to the newest Playboy magazine. They really were a great staff and Blair would be rewarding them for their top-notch service.

She typed in her request for aerobics DVDs and immediately got a return message. "Any specific ones?"

She typed back. "Surprise me."

Within fifteen minutes, she heard a knock on the door. She scurried into the bedroom, heard the door open then close again.

A big blue rubber ball rested near the disabled big screen and a short stack of DVDs lay on the coffee table.

She managed to carry the ball and the DVDs into the bedroom and sorted through them. Romper Room Aerobics had catchy music but the big purple monster's baby talk annoyed her. She couldn't seem to stay on the ball long enough to get through the first set of sit-ups. Besides, her linen shorts kept riding up, cutting her in the crotch and her silk camp shirt kept her from stretching as far as she needed to. The beautiful man and woman on the beach, doing stretches and ogling each other, only made her feel more incarcerated and frustrated than ever.

She wasn't sure how much cardiovascular benefit the last one on the stack could provide, but it had a good soundtrack. Demi Moore and Jamie Lee Curtis seemed to enjoy it. She would give it a try.

CHAPTER ELEVEN

Eric heard vintage Credence Clearwater Revival before he even inserted his key card in the door. The music came from the partially opened bedroom door. The full length mirror reflected so that he could see her, top to bottom.

In her red bra and panties, Selena swayed and ground her hips to the driving music. She was standing on the bed, using the bedpost for her modified pole dance. With her eyes fixed to the television she didn't notice him standing there, watching.

As she wrapped one leg around the bedpost and leaned back letting her head fall backward to touch the mattress, she spotted him.

"Eric!" She let go, tumbling back into the pillows and gasping for breath. She grabbed a pillow and held it in front of her. "I didn't hear you come in."

"I heard there was a really good floorshow here. Glad to see I wasn't misinformed." He grinned at her. "Don't stop on my account."

"I was just...just..." She gestured toward the TV where the pole dancing exercise instructor was now bending from the waist to look at her TV audience upside-down from between her legs.

"Don't let me interrupt." He leaned against the doorframe and crossed his legs to ease the fullness against his fly.

"I was bored." She shrugged and the pillow dropped enough to reveal the lacey cup of her bra.

While he'd seen her in much less, he had never been more affected. "I like the way you keep yourself occupied."

The blondness of her hair made her blush stand out. "For my next act, I rappel down the side of this building disguised as Catwoman. Anything to escape this beautiful prison."

That was his girl. Always quick to recover.

His girl?

All his inner arguments about her not knowing how to play the game crashed and burned as he realized it was him playing all along—and he'd just lost.

Or maybe he'd won the grand prize.

Piano-wire tension dropped from between his shoulder blades as he accepted what he'd been fighting for so long. Selena was his. Now he would make it a fact instead of a fantasy.

"Then I've come to rescue you, my beautiful tiny dancer."

She snorted. "Tiny? Yeah, right. Blowsy, statuesque, voluptuous on a kind day, but never tiny."

"You're perfect." Why couldn't she understand that she was? Her curves defined feminine.

The pillow slipped lower almost to her nipples. Her breasts would be heavy in his hands and overflow, giving him something to squeeze and nuzzle.

"I am the man to set you free." All it would take was one flick of his fingers for him to rid her of that restricting bra. He had to turn away before he offered to do just that. "How do you feel about an afternoon on the water? We could take my sloop out, dock it in a cove and enjoy some sunshine."

"Really? Oh, Eric, that sounds like heaven."

"I think I'm already in heaven." *Could I sound any dorkier?*

Selena gave him a come-hither look stronger than any siren's call.

He pushed away from the doorframe and took a step forward. "Heaven is warmer than I thought it would be. Maybe I'm overdressed."

"You do look a bit flushed. Why don't you take off a few layers and see if that helps?" Selena dropped the pillow. She crawled over to the pillows and began arranging and straightening. Her luscious butt in those red panties wiggled beyond his wildest fantasies. "After all that golfing, you may need to lay down and rest a while."

He peeled off his shirt and dropped it to the floor. The pants took a little more finesse as he carefully unzipped the fly. With a kick of his feet, his shoes went flying with his socks to follow.

Selena watched him from her cocoon of pillows. "There's something about a man undressing that is incredibly sexy."

"Not as sexy as a woman bedpost dancing in red underwear." He climbed onto the bed. "What smells so good in here?"

"Come closer and take a sniff." Welcome, excitement and anticipation glowed from Selena's eyes. And then she licked her lips. Eric's hand started to tremble as he raised it up and ran it over her shoulder.

He leaned in close to her neck and inhaled. "Your scent makes so hot."

The blush started at her breasts, somewhere beyond her bra line, then crept up to her shoulders, her neck, and then colored her cheeks. "And you, sir, set me on fire."

"Then let me help you get some of those restrictive clothes off. We don't want you overheating." Yes! Her bra clasp felt rough on his fingers as he sprang it open. He trailed his fingertips down her back, knowing he would never get his fill of touching her warm, smooth skin.

With Selena, a lifetime wouldn't be long enough to touch her, to taste her, to love her.

She pushed the bra straps from her shoulders and he held each beautiful breast in his hands as he had dreamed of for too many nights. Only this was real. This was now. And he never wanted to go back to dreaming again.

He rubbed his thumbs across her nipples and she gasped.

He swallowed hard before he could ask, "Good?"

"Yes." She wrapped one thigh around him. "More."

He reached down and found panties in the way. "Too many clothes."

"Too many." She quoted back to him as she slid her hand into the waistband of his briefs.

"Me, first." Eric put his hands on her waist, then slowly lowered them to her hips, then slid his hands down her thighs, down her calves and off her feet, rolling her panties off as he explored. By the time he had them off, she was sucking in air and so was he.

Not yet. He wanted more. He wanted...

Selena tugged at his briefs, freeing him from the material that had become much too tight. She brushed the length of him with her palm, then delicately circled his tip with her smallest finger.

In a ragged, throaty whisper, she leaned close and breathed into his ear, "Now?"

More later. Explode now.

No, wait for her. Wait for her. He made it into a litany in his head.

Eric straddled her and Selena opened for him.

Her hands clasped behind his neck, pulling him closer. "Eric, I want you." She bucked up into him, her strong thighs rubbing along his hips. "All of you."

He would give her his soul. He met her half way with his plunge. *Wait for her, wait for her, wait for...*

She squeezed and gave a half squeal, half scream.

His wait was over.

Sparks ignited behind his eyes. Electricity raced through his veins. Colors, sounds, smells, all blurred into one big ball of pure hedonistic pleasure. With a fantastic jolt, ecstasy pulsed through him, throbbing again and again and again, until he poured out the last dregs of his energy into her.

He collapsed onto her, sweat-soaked and spent. When he could catch his breath, he croaked out, "Too heavy?"

"No. Just right." She ran her hands through his hair, along his nape, and over his shoulders. "Just right."

He lifted himself on his elbow. "You, too."

With a great force of willpower, he rolled to her side, breaking their body-to-body connection. She reached for his hand and he threaded his fingers through hers.

He should say something. He should tell her how wonderful he felt when he was around her. He should tell her how beautiful, how brilliant, how important she was to him. He had so much he wanted her to know, but he couldn't make a single word form.

She snuggled her head on his shoulder and he felt a peace greater than any he had ever felt. He would rest, close his eyes and get his thoughts in order.

Give him a few seconds and he would....

As his sleepless nights overcame him, he vowed he would tell her as soon as he woke up.

Selena listened to Eric's breathing become deep and regular. Was he sleeping? He'd fallen asleep on her? She thought about poking him awake but thought that might be the best way to start off this new turn in their relationship.

Relationship. Selena refused to believe it was just two horny, bored people finding relief.

She felt more energized than she had since this charade started. And their midday fantasy beat the hell out of anything she could have planned for tonight. Hurrah for spontaneity! Hurrah for Eric! And hurrah for her, too.

For a few seconds, she tried to nap, too, but she had napped plenty in the last few days and couldn't make herself lay still.

Eric's arm lay under her breasts. The weight felt nice but restrictive. She had to get up.

As she rolled away, his arm tightened and he groaned. Fine. She would stay a few more minutes.

She flopped onto her back and stared at the ceiling, her world spinning faster than if she'd just gotten off the Tilt-A-Whirl.

A fun ride. This was more than that. It had to be.

So this was what the rollercoaster of love felt like. *What do you think, Selena?* she asked herself?

Not think. Thinking could put an end to all this.

Feel. For right now, just feel.

She felt like she never wanted the ride to end.

But all rides end, Selena. Damn. Why couldn't she turn off her brain?

From her heart, she argued that this time was different.

You sure?

She didn't want to hear it. Didn't want to think it.

She sent those thoughts back to the dark and scary place from which they sprang.

But her persistent thoughts cast long shadows. How would this change things between them? After this surreal ride was over, would everyone's life go back to the way it was?

In public, Blair would still be Eric's girlfriend. Nothing there had changed. Would there be any private time for Selena? Would they sneak around, fooling the press—who, thankfully, was proving easily duped? Or would their relationship end when their real lives began again.

They had already enacted this charade for a half a week. How much longer could it last?

Her heart overruled her head. Ride it while you can, Selena Maria. Ride it while you can.

On that resolution, Selena pushed off Eric's one-armed embrace and rolled away. When he groaned, she patted him with a whispered, "Shhh. Go back to sleep. Everything's okay."

And everything would be okay. It always was. Selena was a survivor.

Selena wrapped a towel around her dripping body and ran for the phone. "Hello?"

"Hello? Ms. Blair?"

Damn, she had forgotten. Maybe she had sounded too breathless to be recognizable.

"Hmm?" Hopefully, she sounded unidentifiable and noncommittal enough.

"Mr. Sander's plane is good to go and the limo is here as soon as he is ready."

"Thanks."

Eric was going somewhere? She narrowed her eyes at his sleeping form. Had their lovemaking been goodbye?

Sunshine, he had promised her sunshine.

"Eric?" She trickled her fingers across his chest. "Eric, wake up."

He blinked his hazy blue sleepy eyes and focused. A big happy smile spread across his face. "Hello, beautiful."

Then he sat up, alarm replacing joy. "I didn't mean to fall asleep. I am so sorry. That was horribly rude of me."

"I forgive you if you'll take me on that boat ride you promised me. The concierge called. Your plane is ready. The limo is standing by."

That drove all the sleep from Eric's eyes. "What time is it?" He looked over at the bedside clock. "Do you mind a late lunch? I'll get the cabin stocked and we can munch after we get there. If we don't get going, we might not have much sunshine left to soak up today."

"I don't mind. I've already restocked my candy stash from the minibar so we can nibble on the plane."

"Great. Let me shower, then we'll be out of here." A frown creased his forehead. "I didn't think about needing to pack and check out. We probably want to hang out somewhere else for a while to keep the paparazzi moving."

"I'll take care of the logistics while you shower." Reality kept crashing over her in waves. "It's my job, after all."

With the sound of the shower in the background, Selena fired up her laptop, arranged to have all personal items packed and shipped to Blair's residence and paid all the bills. If Eric wanted to squabble over picking up the check, he could take it up with Blair.

"Did you take care of the publicity setup?" she called to Eric through the door.

"No. I didn't even think about it." The blow-dryer ran for a few seconds, then stopped. "We don't have to, you know. This could be just for us."

Us? If only Selena could count on us. But, in the end, she could only count on herself. "This is a perfect promo op. I'll give the right folks a call."

Blair pushed her white filmy veil off her face and kissed her new husband. "Can you believe we really did it, Dom?"

"Regrets?"

"No. No regrets." She twirled around, arms out like a child. The hot pink ribbons from her white daisy bouquet wrapped around her arms as she grabbed Dominic's hands and coerced him into Ring-around-the-rosy.

"Already leading me in circles, are you?" He picked her up gave her a final twirl and set her down with a kiss that made her think she was still twirling.

Blair had never experienced such sheer happiness. And to think, she had let so many inconsequential things get in her way. Sure, her career was important. But she had forgotten, in all the competition, all the stress, that her true role in the world was musician, not businesswoman. She had become enslaved to the charts, to the media, to everyone but her muses.

And worst of all, she had taken for granted that love would be waiting for her when she figured it out. Thank heavens, Dominic was a patient man.

She stood at the edge of the cliff with Dominic's big hand firmly around her waist. One by one, she picked the petals from her daisies while she chanted, "He loves me, I love him more, he loves me, I love him more."

The wind blew away the tiny petals before they could hit the ground. They danced over the edge of the cliff, swirled on updrafts, then floated into the ocean far below.

The minister, the concierge and the nun from the local convent were her only attendants. They looked on with amusement and discussed the joy of love and the eccentricities of celebrities.

The people behind the barriers, the ones with the cameras, shot photo after photo of the happy couple. She couldn't hear what they discussed, but she bet they were wondering who could file their stories first, which magazine would pay best and who *was* that couple in Palm Springs their duped compadres had been filming for the last few days?

Wouldn't they be surprised to find out that Sister Margaret Elizabeth had already sold her authorized photos to a very credible market for enough money to fill the local food pantries for the next several months?

As the last of the petals fell, Blair gave another fleeting thought to calling Selena and giving her a heads up. When she tried earlier, neither Eric nor Selena answered their cell phones and the room phone kept defaulting to the answering machine. The Majestic had informed Dominic that they didn't give out information on their guests, no matter what security firm he claimed to own.

Right before the ceremony, Dom had somehow found out that they had checked out and they were en route to San Francisco, and that Eric had called ahead to have his sloop prepared for an afternoon outing. Her new husband was a man of great and varied talent.

She gave him another kiss because she couldn't help herself. "Let's go make a baby."

He cocked his eyebrow, and in that good ole' boy accent that melted her insides, drawled back, "I'm up for that."

A quick glance down showed her he told the truth.

"Wife, you're going to have me indecent." He swooped her up so that her dress fell in front of them.

"Husband, I like having you indecent."

With a wave to the crowd, Blair and Dominic slid into the waiting Cadillac. The driver began his circuitous route to the car garage. From there, only Dominic and his staff knew where they were headed to next. But Blair would follow Dominic to the ends of the earth, just as he had done for her for the last few years.

As they would do for each other forever and a day.

CHAPTER TWELVE

As they touched down on the air strip, Selena had to admit that Eric was an excellent pilot. The trip had been mundane, and Selena had relaxed her vigilant watch over the wings and cockpit gauges to enjoy an occasional glimpse of the view.

The trip to the dock was just as uneventful, although the pier was crowded. The day was clear and bright, just right for sunbathing. A towel stretched out on the deck was exactly what she needed to save her sanity after being trapped in that hotel room.

Eric held out his hand to help her from the low slung car. His touch felt warmer, more tender, than before they slept together. How much was real and how much was her imagination?

"Photographers to your left." Eric whispered.

"I see them." Selena held her scarf securely in place as Eric helped her from the Gallardo.

The guard on duty at the private pier gave them a proper nod as they approached, but stared hard at Selena as she passed by him.

Eric's boat was bigger than most apartments Selena had ever lived in, and much better appointed. Teakwood gleamed and smelled of lemon polish. Brass reflected bright light in all directions. The deck chairs had new coverings in heavy navy-and-white canvas.

She followed Eric down the stairway, the hatch he called it, to the stateroom. The room easily accommodated a king-sized bed, a wide dresser and a huge armoire with a full length mirror on the door. Selena couldn't help but wonder how many women had fixed their makeup in that mirror. But she didn't want to know, so she didn't ask.

Eric changed into his swim trunks, modestly using the bathroom for privacy. Of course, he referred to it as the head. Sadly, he preferred a pair of baggy board shorts to a Speedo.

While Selena unpacked her carry-on in the stateroom, Eric went above deck to start the auxiliary motor and pull away from the dock.

She rummaged around in her carry-on until she pulled out two swimsuits. The one-piece fit her perfectly and the cherry-red color would look great with her new hair. The swimsuit would sell well to Blair's fans who still needed their mothers' credit cards—ergo their mothers' approvals—when making their fashion decisions. Although the thigh was cut high, overall, the suit was conservative. Perfect for swimming laps, but not so perfect for vamping.

And vamping was what she wanted to do. After this was all over, she wanted Eric to remember their adventure, to remember her, and salivate. Or at least smile.

It was only fair. She would never forget this slice of time.

The bikini had been one of those last minute additions as she had hastily packed her suitcase. Had it only been a few days ago? It seemed like a lifetime ago instead.

Selena had picked it up on sale a few years ago after being inspired by a travelogue on the French

Riviera but she had never developed the nerve to wear it. Today, she had nerves of steel.

The bottoms were two black crocheted triangles, sewn together at the crotch and tied together with a square knot at the hips. She untied the knots then retied them in easy-off bows instead.

The top was also two crocheted triangles, unlined, so that her nipples peeked through the heavy thread. She tied a loose bow at her neck and another at her back and hoped they would hold until she got on deck. Unless Eric decided to come downstairs first.

The scratchy thread wasn't the most comfortable material against her skin, but then, she wasn't wearing it for comfort. She added impractical strappy mile-high sandals, then checked out her backside view in the full length mirror. The heels lifted her butt nicely.

Eric called down from the stairwell. "I'm cutting the motor now. I think we've got a few cameras off the port side. Ready to come up? You can grab some towels from the closet in the head."

Slipping on a pair of huge Jackie O sunglasses, she gathered up the oversized towels, then strutted across the deck to a sunny portside patch on the deck, fully aware that the photographers were taking photos with their long lenses.

Eric wolf-whistled and she picked up her strut.

"Like what you see?"

Usually so articulate, Eric seemed at a loss for words. "Oh, yeah."

He looked away, then back again, blinking as if expecting her image to change. "Hell, yeah." She'd never worn heels with a swimsuit before. The effect felt very beauty-queenish. As she knelt on all fours to spread her towel, her breasts threatened to spill from the two small triangles covering them, especially when she reached as far as she could to straighten a corner of the towel that didn't need smoothing out. *That* little act was for Eric's benefit. Looking up beneath her eyelashes, she felt empowered when he responded nicely.

His voice was deeper than usual when he said, "Let me help with that."

He knelt down next to her, brushing his shoulder into hers as he pushed at the towel.

"Thanks." Selena took her time lowering herself to the deck, trying to be graceful despite her quivering of nerves inside. She lay on her stomach and raised up on an elbow, which plumped her breasts in their flimsy restraints.

Not yet, girls. Don't pop out yet.

Eric's upper lip beaded in sweat.

She licked her lips. "You know what would be nice?" She enjoyed watching his Adam's apple bob as he swallowed.

"What?"

"If you would spread this oil on me." Clichéd maybe, but who needed originality when the classic move had withstood the hands of time?

Eric poured the oil into his hands and rubbed it to warm it. His long, strong fingers kneaded the oil into her skin, working at the muscles knotted between her shoulder blades, right where her bikini top string was knotted, too. Just one pull. Would he do it?

"Mmm." A groan escaped her at the sensuousness of it all. Eric's strong hands paused before rubbing lower on her hips.

She took a deep breath to calm herself. The strain threatened to loosen her back tie. Had Eric noticed? Selena looked up at him, knowing he couldn't read her expression behind her dark sunglasses.

His face was easier to interpret. He had the same look as the teenaged captain of the high school football team when he got to cop his first feel all those years ago. The sophomore hadn't gotten lucky that night, but that was then and this was now. Eric would get lucky today and he knew it.

"Would you untie the knots? I don't want a tan line now, do I?"

"No, we couldn't have that." He pulled the back tie and the bow at the back of her neck.

Selena pulled the top from underneath her. Surprisingly, knowing about the cameras gave her an extra tingle. Excitingly, knowing that Eric watched made her burn.

He poured more oil into his hands. "The swimsuit isn't the only one with knots." He straddled her so that his knees touched each side of her waist. With strong thumbs, he rubbed the knots from her back, gently smoothing from spine to ribs.

Again, she groaned, low and long. "Your hands are magic hands."

Eric's arousal brushed against her leg. "Yeah? My hands are nothing compared to my magic wand." His fake sexy tone was underlaid by a very real sexiness.

She laughed at his corniness. This was the Eric she knew and loved. *Yes, loved.* Under his hands, warmed by the sun, she didn't have the willpower to deny it to herself right now.

"Magic wand, huh? Does that make you a magician?"

"Oh, yeah, baby. You wouldn't believe the magic acts I can perform. I've got a stage performance that's got to be lived to be believed."

"Then I'll be your willing starlet-accomplice." She turned over, surprising him. She peeped over the top of her glasses so he could see that she studied very inch of him. Under her scrutiny, the bulge in his swimsuit grew until it bumped her very sensitive mound.

His gaze left her body long enough to glance in the direction of the distant cameras, then went back to her. "I'm going to kick myself in the morning for this, but, did you forget about the paparazzi?"

"No. I didn't forget. Haven't you always wanted to be on camera?"

He shivered and his eyes went dark as the idea became reality. "Let the show begin."

"Tell me, Mr. Magician, can you mesmerize me?"

"I think you've already performed that trick on me." He rubbed his palms over her peaked nipples. "But you can make my marionette dance if you want."

"I think we've got too many strings between us for that." She untied the bows at each hip and the bottom triangles parted. She raised her pelvis to pull the scrap of material from underneath her, rubbing herself against him as she prolonged the task. "Swimsuit lines can be such a bitch to get rid of."

"Quite right. We wouldn't want unseemly lines." Pure male appreciation for her was evident in every inch of his body.

She hooked her thumbs into his swimsuit and pulsed up against him. "You don't want an unsightly tan line, do you?"

"No," he gasped. "No tan lines."

He lay flat on her as he pushed off his trunks with his legs. His sinuous movements had her gasping in passion. He raised up on his knees barely high enough so that his chest hair tickled her erect nipples. "I'm not too heavy, am I?"

"No. Oh, no." The primeval urge to surge had her thrusting her hips up into his.

"Easy." He kissed her neck. "You want to make the most of your moment in the spotlight, don't you?"

The thought of an unknown voyeur capturing all this on film almost made her come right then. She panted, trying to pace herself. "Make it last."

"I'll do my best, madam." Eric's voice choked with need. He grabbed the bottle and drizzled warm, thick oil over her breasts. With a lazy finger on one breast, he made a slow spiral of circles, tighter and tighter as he neared the peak. With each rotation, he pushed her closer and closer to the edge.

She pushed her breast against his hand but he pulled back.

"Not yet, starlet." He circled the air above her sensitized nipple, not quite touching it. Then he started on her other breast, even more slowly than the first one. As he circled, he whispered, "I could use some oil myself. Wouldn't want to burn, would I?"

As she reached for the bottle, just beyond her fingertips, he grabbed it up and poured more oil on her aching breast. "Now you can reach it."

With a shaking hand, she rubbed oil from her own breast, almost climaxing as she brushed across her sensitive peak.

He nipped her ear. "You're not following the script. On my count, my beautiful apprentice. We don't want to rush the timing, do we?"

"Noooooooo." Try as she might, she couldn't help but plunge against him. She had never had this much unfulfilled need before.

He lifted up so that the tip of his penis barely touched her swollen mound as he looked into her face. "So beautiful. So damned beautiful."

"I'm ready for our grand *finale*." She reached down and squeezed ever so firmly, then she guided him in.

Strain showed in his neck as he kept himself raised above her, still and waiting.

She caught his hips and pulled him into her. An overwhelming wave swept through her and she screamed out his name.

Above her, his eyes closed and his throat strained as he dropped his head back. "Love youuuuuuuuuuuuuu."

Wave after wave hit her, as every muscle in her body pulsed.

Eric throbbed within her as she clenched around him, both of them jerking with ungraceful spasms of exhilarating release.

Finally, he collapsed on her, then struggled to raise himself on an elbow, his face flushed and his eyes dreamy.

She looked up at him and grinned. "That, my dear, was one hell of a standing ovation."

"Yeah." The man so usually glib with words had been reduced to monosyllables.

Selena felt proud as well as satisfied.

Damn, she was good.

Eric watched as Selena showered. When she raised her arms to shampoo her hair, he nearly came undone even after his recent release. God, he loved her. He'd been attracted to her since the first time he saw her, but now—now, he didn't know how he could ever live without her.

They should talk. Not like they hadn't already, all those hours at the hotel, but they had talked about their pasts, about past boyfriends and ex-wives and parents or lack thereof. But they had carefully avoided mentioning anything to do with their futures. Selena avoided all mention of a future, with or without him. Whenever he tried to turn the conversation, she had turned it back.

But now, he wanted more.

Over a good meal and an excellent glass of wine, he would ask her about her dreams, her aspirations, her feelings for him. And he damned well intended to make her understand his feelings for her, no matter how hard she tried to evade him. If he kept his love for her bottled up too much longer, he might burst.

"I think I used all the hot water." She wrapped a towel draped around her as she entered the stateroom. The slit in her makeshift sarong opened and closed all the way up her thigh as she walked. She had the sexiest legs.

"I don't need hot water. You make me hot just looking at you."

The smile she answered him with took his breath away. Pure, unguarded happiness sparkled from her eyes. It was a look few would ever get to see and he felt privileged.

She picked up the gel, looked at the jar, then put it down again. "I think I'll skip the goo tonight. How Blair stands to have that slimy stuff on her scalp, I will never understand."

"Good. I like the silky way your hair feels *au naturel*. In fact, I like the way all of you feels *au naturel*." He hoped she would drop the towel.

Instead she said, "You hungry?"

"I could eat. I can call ahead and get a private dining room in the city." Tonight would be a good time to start having those long talks.

She walked toward him, her bare feet leaving damp footprints and her towel parting and closing as she took each step. "I took a peek in your fridge and in your pantry. If you can live on crackers and cheese and chilled, boiled shrimp, we could eat out here on the water, couldn't we?"

"Sure. But it will be too dark to troll in if we stay past sunset. I've got running lights, but I don't like to sail in the dark. The docks get too crowded to bring her in without risking a nudge from another boat."

"Could we anchor here overnight? Maybe even sleep out under the stars?"

"Yeah, we could do that." *Thank you, Fates.* "I'll set up a table on the deck."

"Couldn't we lug up these big pillows instead? I'd really like to, you know, get decadent." She blushed, actually blushed for him.

"I love the way you think." He put his arms around her. "And the way you smell. And the way you kiss. And the way you move. And the way you breathe. And..."

Her stomach growled. "And my appetite?"

"Yeah, baby. I love your appetite, too, especially if I'm included on your menu."

"Hmmm. Maybe for dessert." She turned out of his embrace and picked up the stack of pillows. "Dessert's the best part of the meal, don't you think?"

On the dresser, Eric's cell phone vibrated. The neon light blinked frantically, signally numerous messages. Eric glanced at it, then up at the stairs.

Selena watched it dance on the dresser top. "You should answer it. We can keep the real world at bay for only so long."

Eric sighed and surrendered to the inevitable.

While he checked his messages, Selena took a much needed breath. Sooner or later she would have to think about that declaration of love he'd shouted out in the middle of his climax. He'd thrown that love word around fairly liberally ever since.

She had never said it. Not to anyone. Ever. She wasn't sure she could. She'd never wanted to say it before, but now she did. She wanted to say it to Eric but fear clogged her throat.

Eric's brow crinkled as he listened to his messages. When he clicked off the phone, his eyes radiated worry. "I've got bad news."

"Your grandmother?"

"No. Blair."

Selena's heart skipped a beat and she felt lightheaded. "Tell me."

"She and Dominic got married."

Blood rushed back into her head with a vengeance, giving her a pounding headache. "But that's good news." She lobbed a pillow at him. "I was so worried."

Eric didn't even crack a smile. "Photos of the happy couple are all over the news. There's even an interview, although Grandmumsy hasn't heard it yet."

"Oh." Selena suddenly felt very naked and silly in her heels. She wrapped her towel around her. "Do you know any more?"

"Yeah. Grandmumsy says my car is being staked out by the media. She and her driver are at the dock with her Towncar. They're parked as close as they can get, but she says there's still quite a gauntlet to run through." Eric looked at the waning sun. "I don't have the light to take us to another pier."

"No. I'm not running." Selena stared out to sea. "We knew that our masquerade could be unmasked when we started this. Part of my job is damage control. I'll say something about privacy and love and marriage and—oh, I don't know what I'll say but I'll make it work."

"Blair has no idea what a treasure you are. I can't believe she did this to us."

Selena watched Eric with bleak eyes. "To you. My reputation is expendable. I'm a nobody. But you've worked too hard to build respect for Walking Hill. Let me go first and distract them. I'll say—I'll think of something.... I'll move them away from the car. While they're distracted, you make a break for the car. I'll take a taxi or rent a car or something and head back to Blair's when I can."

Eric looked as if he might argue, but the sloop bucked and he had to turn his attention back to his piloting.

Selena dressed in a runway-worthy sundress and stared at the parody of Blair in the mirror. She gave herself a good mental shake. *You've stared down a crowd before, girl. Remember. No fear.*

The end of the dock was crowded.

"Paparazzi." Eric said.

"Paparazzi with piranha appetites." Selena took a deep breath and prepared to disembark. "Let the feeding frenzy begin."

Eric took a firm hold on her elbow. "Together, we'll make a hell of a mouthful."

CHAPTER THIRTEEN

"Scared?" Eric asked.   Selena looked at the mob twenty yards away, held back by a single, thin security guard. "A little."

Eric reached for her hand. His was warm and large enough to swallow hers up. She'd never noticed that about his hands before. Nor had she ever experienced the surge of strength and courage he gave her. It started in her fingers and spread up through her arm to her heart.

"We'll get through this." He gave her hand a squeeze.

Since she couldn't speak past the knot in her throat, she nodded her agreement. This might be the wildest ride she had ever ridden.

She came to a stop behind the security guard at the end of the pier. All that separated her from them was a small, wrought iron gate that just reached her knees. No podium to hide behind, no microphone to speak over the noise. She felt so exposed.

"Give us a smile," someone yelled.

A smile was more than she could manage. She would settle for poised right now. Of course, Eric looked great. He smiled to the crowd and most of them smiled back. Cameras flashed and popped as he gave them a little wave.

She should say something, but what? The paparazzi were beginning to shuffle their feet as if they were finding traction to begin a charge.

"Thanks for coming out today." With that one little sentence, Eric owned them. They all fell still and silent, waiting to see what he would say next.

Now that he had taken control, he put his arm around Selena's waist and said, "On behalf of Blair and her new husband, we want to thank you for all the good wishes they have received."

A camera flashed, breaking Eric's spell.

"How do you feel about Blair marrying another man?"

"Blair's one of my best friends. I'm very happy for her and for her husband."

"Is it true that her husband is her long time body guard?"

"Yes. The situation is a classic, straight from the movies, isn't it?" Eric chattered back and forth, so at ease. That grin at the corner of his mouth might even mean he was enjoying himself.

"Is she pregnant?"

"I wouldn't know. I really mean it when I say that Blair and I are just friends." His quip brought a chuckle throughout the crowd.

"Are you and Blair's assistant only friends, too?"

Eric's grin stiffened, but only those close to him could have seen it. And Selena was very, very close. She held her breath, waiting for his answer.

"Friends." He gave her a brotherly hug around the shoulders. "Just friends."

Selena felt her heart sink to her stomach.

"What is the purpose of her assistant masquerading as her?"

She should have never forgotten, not for a single second, that this whole experience was a big game of charades. The few times she'd ever played, she had always lost. Looked like history was repeating itself.

Eric showed that crowd-pleasing smile, bright and shiny. "As many of you know, Selena often stands in for fittings for Blair. She also stands in for video rehearsals. Presently, she is supporting Blair's new clothing line." Eric pulled Selena in front of him. "Doesn't she look great?"

Eric began to clap, looked over to the security guard who caught the look and also began to clap and effectively started the whole crowd whooping and clapping in appreciation.

Eric had more star quality charisma in his little pinkie than most actors had in their whole bodies.

One of the reporters on the front row yelled, "What are you wearing, Selena?"

While working on Blair's summer line, Selena had heard the fashion patter so often that the canned phrases popped into her head. "I'm wearing a ruffle-bottomed slipdess in vavoom-red, with chunky earrings and bracelets to match. The strappy sandals, also in vavoom- red, give the whole thing an extra kick. This ensemble will be available in Blair's summer line out May twenty-second."

Amidst flashing bulbs, she attempted a turn like she'd seen the high fashion models do. As she bobbled on the end, Eric caught her elbow and held her steady. She made herself pull away. Only a few days ago, distancing herself from his touch would have been instinctive instead of painful. But she needed to stand on her own two feet. *Just friends* sounded nothing like *I love you*. Eric might have said it for the crowd, but then again....

Eric lifted on his toes, focused over the crowd and nodded, movements so subtle that Selena wouldn't have noticed if she hadn't been hyperaware of him.

Four young men dressed in matching khakis and polo shirts headed for the end of the pier where Selena and Eric stood. Even without their tuxedoes, Grandmere's boy toys made a statement.

Two of them stopped directly in front of Selena and Eric and two of them fell in behind.

"Let's go." Eric put his hand on her shoulder and reached across to thread the fingers of his other hand through hers. Behind her, the waiter-cum-escort put his hand on her shoulder and closed the gap between them. Selena was effectively cocooned between him and Eric and the man in front.

She'd seen Blair pull off this maneuver a thousand times and had always thought that she might trip and fall with the slightest misstep, as close as they were. But Eric kept such a firm grip that should she stumble, he could right her without breaking stride.

When the crowd swarmed around them, Selena thought she would get claustrophobic but she didn't. Instead, the excitement energized her, making her feel like she was dropping from the highest peak of Paramount's The Beast.

As if they had practiced many times, the driver opened the car door and her escorts parted to let her through. Eric untangled his hands and offered her an open palm to help her climb into the car. She ducked and scooted across the seat, and Eric climbed in beside her and shut the door.

He let out a breath. "Are you all right?"

"Wow! That was something, wasn't it? I can see how you and Blair could get off on that kind of thrill."

The escorts peeled off and melted into the crowd. Selena sent them a silent thank-you and wished them well.

Selena untangled her fingers from Eric's as she buckled her seatbelt. It was a good reason to create some distance between them.

"You did great, Selena." He reached for her hand.

"Thanks. We both did pretty well, I think." The adrenaline was starting to drain from her, leaving her depleted and head-achy.

The driver, the major domo from the party, spoke from the front seat. "A crowd that big could have easily turned into a mob."

"Yeah." Eric lay his head against the high seatback. As poised as he was, the situation must have played on his nerves, too.

The driver eased through the crowd then headed for the freeway and home. But home alone would be so lonely now.

"Just friends, huh?" Selena had meant it to be a flirty question in a teasing voice. Instead it was bitter and sad, with Eric's *Love you* still ringing in her ears.

Without being asked, the driver pushed a button to put up a partition between him and them.

"What do you think?" Eric's tone was sharper than hers. His eyes were narrowed. His jaw was clenched. He was livid.

Selena stared. She'd never even seen him grumpy, much less angry. What did it mean? Her heart told her that she had insulted him, but her head said that maybe he thought she was trying to trap him.

"No. You first." Selena hoped Eric could read the fear behind her bravado.

Eric frowned, opened his mouth, then closed it again. Then he picked up one of her hands. "All those visits to Blair's out of town concerts, all those late nights and early mornings at her place—they were for you. I couldn't stay away. I tried. For days, sometimes even a whole week, I could stay away. But then, the days would get too long, the sun too dim and I would need my Selena-fix."

Absently, he rubbed his thumb across hers. "I thought it was infatuation, that it would go away. But it hasn't. I'm certain now that it never will."

He paused until she looked at him. "I love you, Selena. "I have always loved you. I will always love you."

Her heart shouted, *I love you, too*. Now was the perfect time. How hard was it to say?

She couldn't make the L-word form in her mouth. Love was nice to think about. Nice to enjoy when commitment wasn't involved. But now? It was real and it was very, very frightening. A thousand times more frightening than a volatile mob of paparazzi.

Finally, after the moment had passed, she choked out, "I believe you."

Eric reacted like she'd just sucker-punched him. She guessed he probably felt that way, too. She wanted to explain, but she couldn't. She didn't know what she wanted to say.

She looked out the window to break eye-contact. The Big Sur exit loomed ahead.

She pressed the intercom button and said to the driver, "Turn there." She pointed. "Turn off at Big Sur. I need to think."

The driver peeled off, squeezing between a minivan and a cop on a motorcycle. He must have been a race car driver in his younger days. The paparazzi was left behind.

Selena gave directions to the amusement park. Eric stared out his own window, stiff and silent.

The driver pulled to the entrance of the park. For the first time since she met him, Eric didn't rush to open the door for her. She guessed he was right. It was her turn this time.

Selena climbed out of the car and walked to Eric's side. She opened his door. "Are you coming with me?"

He gave her a wary look, then exited. He was tense as if he expected her to double up her fist and land one to his stomach any minute. But then, she'd already done that figuratively.

She flashed her pass and they both walked through the gates. Unfaltering, she kept a quick pace to the Giant Dipper. She needed to think. No! She needed to stop thinking. Outside of sex with Eric, a hard and fast ride was the best technique she knew of.

The line was short, no more than a dozen people. At the ticket counter, the boy on the cash register did a double take. "Selena?"

"New look." She shoved money through the cage. "Two please."

Next to her, Eric jerked. Before he could say anything, she pushed through the turnstile. She gave a wave to the attendants as she walked to the back car. Eric held back at the front of the train.

"Come on." She called him over.

As he came up beside her, she ushered him in. "After you."

He climbed in and she climbed in beside him and pulled the safety bar down. The chains caught under the cars and they lurched forward. Up and up they crawled. Inch by inch, Selina left old fears and hurts behind her. This was how it always worked, as if she could leave behind her scarred past and see into the future. She usually looked for a future without baggage, without responsibility, without anyone but herself to worry about.

As they climbed to the peak, Selena covered Eric's hand with her own.

For the first time since his impassioned speech in the car, he looked at her instead of past her.

Over the clanking of the pulleys, she said, "I've been afraid all my life. But when I'm with you, I'm not afraid anymore."

Eric didn't fall into her arms, but he didn't pull away either. He did exactly what she hoped he would do. He waited for her to be ready.

They made their first swooping curve then picked up speed for the big hill. The higher they went, the closer Selena came to freedom.

This time, freedom didn't mean ties with nobody and nothing. This time, freedom meant more than leaving her past behind. This time, freedom meant rushing toward the future she hoped to have, a future with Eric. Without him, the future would be flat and dull and empty of all excitement.

The chains clanked and strained as they pushed the cars to the climax. For a split-second, at the peak everything stood still.

Then it came, over the top. As they dropped, Selena's heart won over her head. From deep inside her, she shouted, "Eric, I love you."

The ride down felt more exhilarating than any plunge she'd ever taken.

Eric fought against g-forces to wrap her in his arms. "I love you back."

Through the whole ride, Selena squeezed Eric's hand and laughed and screamed. Tears streamed down her face as they slung around curves and fell down hills, defying gravity. And through it all, she yelled, over and over again, "I love you, I love you, I love you!"

The only time she'd ever had a better four and a half minutes was when she and Eric had had a lot less clothes on. Then, she'd felt the words. But now, she could say them. "I love you."

"I love you, too." He kissed her, deep and full.

As the car came to a stop, she wiped away her tears. "You need to know what you're getting. My whole life has been one wild ride. It's been dark and scary sometimes, too."

Eric wrapped her in his arms. "I promise, you'll never ride without me again."

Thanks so much for purchasing White Wine & Wild Rides! Readers like you are why writers like me can share our stories.

Want to share your comments and opinions about this story? See the next page for hints and suggestions.

If you enjoyed, **White Wine & Wild Rides**, please spread the love.

Review

Please, share your opinion by leaving a review on our favorite bookseller site or on Goodreads.com (and thanks in advance. Your comments mean the world to me.)

Twitter

Give a tweet, include me(@ConnieCox), and I'll RT!

Facebook

I'm a facebook junkie(facebook.com/Connie.Cox) and/or facebook.com/ConnieCox.writer). I'd love to add a comment or a *like* if you add me to your post.

Now I'll share with you—

New Release Notification

Want to know when my next story is available?

Sign up for my newsletter at www.ConnieCox.com (Occasionally, I give stuff away to my newsletter subscribers, too.)

Sneak Peek

Have you read **Contractually Yours**?

What's it about? A wedding planner must marry a very wealthy jilted groom or her parents will lose their home. If she doesn't keep it strictly business, she will loose her heart.

For a sneak peek—just turn the page!
Sneak Peak

CONTRACTUALLY YOURS

CHAPTER 1

"The wedding is off, Brandon D'Estrehan announced as dispassionately as if he were ordering a cup of coffee. "My apologies for the inconvenience."

For the hundredth time in two days, Caroline Duplessis pushed replay on the DVD player to study the video of the world's most respected and feared international corporate raider calling off his wedding from the altar rail.

The wedding photographer in the vestibule had picked up his deep baritone clearly in the huge St. Louis Cathedral in the heart of New Orleans' French Quarter. D'Estrehan had looked over the diamond-bedecked crowd as expressionless as if his face were chiseled from the same stone his heart must have been carved from.

She zoomed in to study his eyes. No blink. No flicker. Nothing but black irises in dark brown pupils staring out over the distinguished crowd.

Ruthless. The guests had called him cold-blooded and ruthless as they filed out of the church.

Caroline just called him 'dream killer.'

From the tabloids, she knew the groom had gone back to business as usual that very evening. The heart-broken bride could not be found.

Caroline glanced down at the sheaf of bills and her extremely small bank balance spread across the coffee table that doubled as her make-shift desk in her home-office. Her studio apartment wasn't big enough for a proper desk, even if she could have afforded one. No other way around it, the end of this wedding meant the end of her fledging wedding planning service, Weddings Divine.

ABOUT THE AUTHOR

Books have always been Connie Cox's passion. Many thanks to her mom for that! Connie used to think authors were sophisticated creatures who lived in NYC, went to glitzy parties and wrote as the muse dictated. Then she met one. The writer looked a lot like her-jeans, a few extra pounds, a love of books and a quirky imagination.

Connie's newfound love for running is taking care of the extra pounds. Her fascination with Jungian psychology takes care of her story lines. And her innate wild imagination does the rest.

People fascinate Connie, especially people who fall in love. Writing romance novels gives Connie the freedom (a lot of freedom!)to explore the chemistry that brings lovers together. It's an exploration Connie takes seriously as she looks into that sexual spark that turns two singles into a couple. Her story people really have to work hard for that coupling as she sends her characters on a journey of discovery both within themselves and in each other. But the happily ever after makes the journey worth it. And there are often a few laughs along the way.

So why does Connie write? Because, now that she's discovered the magic of letting loose the people in her imagination, she's impossible to be around if she doesn't let them have their way!

With many thanks for the encouragement of that first writer and many who have followed behind her, Connie now lives the dream, writing big stories from her little desk in her little Louisiana town. Even as you read this, she is working on a new story and living her own happily ever after.